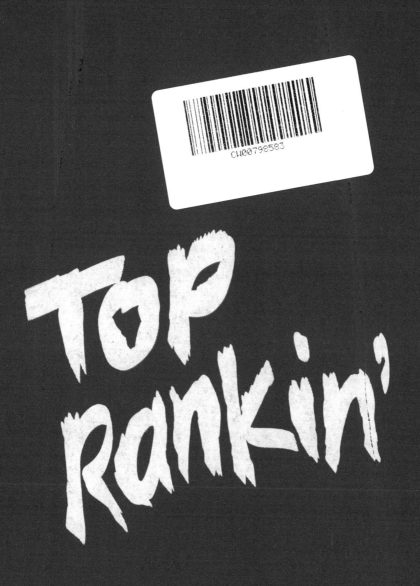

RARE BIRD
LOS ANGELES, CALIF.

Top Rankin'

A PUNK/SKA NOIR NOVEL

HOWARD PAAR

author of Once Upon a Time in LA

Publisher's Cataloging-in-Publication data

Names: Paar, Howard, author.
Title: Top rankin' : a punk / ska noir novel / Howard Paar.
Description: First Trade Paperback Original Edition | A Genuine Rare Bird
Book | New York, NY; Los Angeles, CA: Rare Bird Books, 2021.
Identifiers: ISBN: 9781644281932
Subjects: LCSH Ska (Music)—Fiction. | Punk rock music—California—Fiction.
| Los Angeles (Calif.)—History—20th century—Fiction. | Music trade—United
States—Fiction. | Noir Fiction. | BISAC FICTION / General | FICTION / Noir
Classification: LCC PS3616.A23 T67 2021 | DDC 813.6—dc23

To my brilliant editors, Denise Hamilton and Sonja Bolle, both of whom were on the O.N. Klub dance floor. Denise, you told me the day we met when I was starting *Once Upon a Time in LA* that I should write this story and I never would have but for you.

IN MEMORY OF:

Clyde Grimes	Graham Price
Louise Monty	Ranking Roger
Stuart Kleinman	Darby Crash
Joe Strummer	Ellen Levine
Suzanne Macnary	Pucci Rosser
Larry Monroe	Mary Byrne
Chris Murphy	

CREDITS:
Faith Evans, copyeditor

Sequential soundtrack available on Spotify. Play Loud!

CHAPTER 1

1979

JAMES DUAL SAT ON the Sunset Strip outside the deco double doors of the run-down, now-glorified crash pad, Sunset Tower apartment building, on the steps that everyone from Jean Harlow and Paulette Goddard to Frank Sinatra and Ava Gardner had walked up in the joint's illustrious past, wondering what the fuck he'd do next. The record label job contract he'd landed fresh off the boat from London would mercifully expire at midnight but "broke" would follow soon after. He wished the cops who were a by-product of his time at Real Records would expire too.

On the upside, he had found some really tasty Levi's STA-PREST trousers yesterday at Poseur on Hollywood Boulevard and some narrow red 1/4" braces at the Army & Navy store on Vine to hold them up high above the lace-up black English officer's boots he sported these days.

He'd been told about a guy who owned a failing club and was looking for someone to rescue things but hadn't picked up the phone yet.

Despite all this, he was waiting on wild child actor spawn Drea Dresden, well aware that they caused a lot more trouble together than apart, but neither of the sometime-lovers could resist.

Ten minutes later, she banged out through the Sunset Tower's doors, black lace top half off one shoulder, holding a rapier lazily in her left hand. There appeared to be a bit of dried blood on the tip.

He looked up at her as she offered a hand to elevate his hungover ass, her black hair draping across him. A club owner had once described her as Stevie Nicks if she'd been raised by the Manson family but he would have said a young Gloria Swanson.

"Rough night?" he asked.

"Not particularly. Leslie and I hung out with these two old film writer guys who had good coke. They gave up trying to fuck us about three a.m. and weren't too boring with their stories about what this place used to be like," she said in her signature ironic, husky voice.

"Is that blood on the rapier?"

"Yeah. It was from an old Errol Flynn movie one of the guys had written and he had it mounted on the wall. I used it to demonstrate what would happen if he touched my ass again."

"Does Iggy Pop still live here?"

He'd heard tales that he used to dive out of his apartment window into the pool way below.

"Iggy's a fucking mess. Why do you even care?"

"'Cause he fucking counts, Drea. *Raw Power*, especially, is a crucial record. In London, I'd put stereo speakers either side of my head and play it at full volume to blast a hangover into next week."

"Honey, as good as that record is, I've seen him passed out on his face too many times to say he's crucial."

He let it go, knowing his London perspective wasn't as up-close as hers. "Want to get some breakfast?"

"Yeah. I'm starving."

"Denny's or the Tropicana?"

"Let's go to Schwab's or Greenblatt's. They're nearer."

They were walking, which was just as well for the citizens of West Hollywood. James had been limo'd around for the last two years and no one, including Drea, thought it wise to give her a driver's license. They ambled down Sunset to Crescent Heights and grabbed a couple of counter spots at Schwab's Pharmacy, a legendary spot that had been open since 1932. The joint had a lovely rep for having catered to actors, including Orson Welles, Judy Garland, the Marx Brothers, and Marilyn Monroe, but also treated "under employed" hopefuls with the same deference, which extended to the odd free meal. James had become intrigued by the place as a kid watching Billy Wilder's *Sunset Boulevard* when a broke William Holden heads to "headquarters," the place where everyone meets to wait for the "gravy train."

Drea unhooked her black purse from the bullet belt that crossed from right shoulder to left waist, pulling out a furled newspaper. "Here, I got you the new *NME* from the Cahuenga newsstand yesterday."

"Fuck, thanks."

They ordered from a waitress who probably dated from when a broke Ava Gardner worked there while waiting for her big break: James, the pork chop and eggs; Drea, the eggs Benedict.

He opened the English music newspaper so they could both leaf through. "Look—the Only Ones are coming to do multiple nights at the Whisky."

The food came quickly as always and, seeing him fully engrossed in dipping a crispy bite of pork chop into egg yolk, she turned the page.

"Hey, look at these guys. They're dressed exactly like you are today except you don't have a porkpie hat."

The Specials' debut single "Gangsters" is coming out on their own 2 Tone label, read the caption below the band picture.

"Fuck, I need to hear that. Let's eat quick. Tower might have it but if not, I bet Aron's on Melrose will."

An hour later, after striking out going through Tower's fairly well-stocked racks of import 7" vinyl, the mission was accomplished at Aron's Records. He got a shiver of anticipation looking at the stunning black-and-white label logo and instinctively loved the idea of putting a different band, The Selecter, on the flip side. They hustled over to Drea's place on Kilkea and dropped it on her battered turntable.

The instant, pure adrenaline rush was indescribable and two minutes and forty-eight seconds later, he knew he'd just heard the future. It was about to be 1980 and this was what he wanted it to sound like.

CHAPTER 2

JAMES WALKED OUT OF the February 1980, mid-afternoon Sunset Strip heat into the gloom of Filthy McNasty's, a small club he'd rarely bothered with although he had heard that the Johnny Ortega band from his beloved childhood *77 Sunset Strip* TV series had rehearsed there.

He was there to meet Bob Selva, the co-owner of this spot and apparently another joint that was hurting.

The place had that funky smell all closed clubs have in the daytime. He shook hands with the fortyish, stocky, balding guy who wore a satin baseball jacket, black pants, and well-polished shoes.

Selva pointed to the unattended bar. "Can I get you something?"

"Nah. I'm alright, thanks."

They retired to a small booth in the gloom. After minimal small talk, Selva got to the point.

"I've got a club, the Oriental Nights, that's struggling, and I hear you might be on top of what new punk bands are coming up. I've had a Vietnamese restaurant and bar thing going but it's on its last legs."

"I've spent a lot of time seeing everyone who's playing at the moment but I'm getting bored with most of them. They are all starting to sound the same to me. Even the clothes and hair are starting to turn into some identikit uniform."

"Who cares, if you can pack people in?"

James, for once, kept his musical temper in check. "Here's the thing. I have been thinking a lot about what would make me excited to go to a club other than a specific band, and when I heard the song 'Gangsters' last year, it crystalized things for me. See, the Whisky, for instance, is booking great bands but the music between bands doesn't match. Like, you go in to see, say, Elvis Costello or the Ramones but some fucking hippy soundman is playing the Doobie Brothers or some such shit before the band goes on. Kills your buzz right there. When I heard the Specials' 'Gangsters,' it was all clear to me. Injecting the adrenaline of punk and revving up old ska music is a genius idea. They also packed out the Whisky for four shows here, so there's interest.

"I'm thinking create more of a dance club, play ska and soul, and just have one band a night that matches that. Instead of cramming in three bands a night, seven nights a week like fucking Madame Wong's, just open Friday and Saturday night so it feels like an event, right?

"Also, talking of Wong's, you gotta change the name. It makes me think of her place or the Hong Kong Cafe."

Selva smiled at the Londoner's enthusiasm but said, "Two nights a week won't be enough in the long run but maybe it could start that way. And I can't afford to do a name change. You really think kids will want this?"

"The cool ones will. The South Bay hardcore punk thing is shifting things too. All the jock cunts who were playing high school football six months ago are jumping on the bandwagon and into the mosh pit. It's boring to me. And do you want to be dealing with that head-cracking violent shit every night?"

An hour later, Selva rose and offered his hand. "Okay, let's try it, James. By the way, did you really kill that band, the Confederacy?"

"Yeah. I hated that long-haired, Confederate flag-waving, guitar-soloing shit-kicker music. They deserved to die," James said with dripping punk irony. But he felt a nagging pain inside again for the girl he'd lost that night.

"You are wiry, blond, spiky-haired, and what, maybe five foot nine or ten, and look more like you should be in an English band, not running a club in LA. I'd say not dangerous, but those ice-cold blue eyes have a dark look in them, like you know things no one else does. I wouldn't want to fuck with you."

"Do you think I'd be walking the streets of Hollywood right now if the FBI high-tech investigation showed I had anything to do with that crash?"

Selva let his bomber jacket fall open, revealing a shoulder holster and hefty pistol. "The club business isn't for the faint of heart, especially in Silver Lake. Just wanted to make sure you can handle yourself."

CHAPTER 3

JAMES AND DREA TOOK the RTD bus east on Sunset and were dropped a block west of Silver Lake Boulevard. It was early evening and there were few people on the street in the largely Hispanic neighborhood. They walked the block, looking for 3037 and mistakenly walked into a gay bar called the Cave before seeing the very run-down place that was built into the hillside. It had a big set of red, Spanish-looking double doors that were padlocked, but they spotted a smaller single door, which Selva had said would be opened with the key he had entrusted to James. He looked at her and grinned.

"Kind of exciting, huh?"

He got the door open and stepped into the darkness, fumbling along the wall, looking for any kind of light switch. He could hear scurrying noises within. Other than a couple of rats, the light revealed that they were in a tiny entryway, with a cashier's window on the left. Pulling a tatty curtain aside led them into the oblong room. A wooden bar ran along the left and the very low stage was set up on the right.

There were a couple of circular pillars at either side of the open dance floor. Selva's words came back to him: "DID YOU REALLY KILL THAT BAND?"

Almost two years later, and the long quizzical looks still followed him like a comet tail he couldn't shake. He'd been hired by Real Records, who wanted to buy his punk energy and insight, soon after

14

he'd arrived in LA, aiming to escape the horrible social-economic situation in London. His obsession with authenticity had led to a brutal culture clash with an American record industry still drenched in Quaaludes and white wine consumed to the sound of the Eagles, Fleetwood Mac, and Peter Frampton while James was fueled by amphetamines and the Clash. He'd advocated offing out-of-date and underselling bands like the Confederacy in great detail at a career-ending company meeting, so when the band's plane had crashed after leaving LA and sabotage was discovered, he became a suspect. Eventually, the FBI had accepted there was no physical proof of his involvement. That and the fact that he was alibied up all night with his colleagues at the band's Roxy show and then after with Sue Ann, the backup singer he was falling for—right until she walked up the plane's steps to her death—meant he was still on the streets. He forced all thoughts of her back to that sad, dark corner of his mind, as he knew this club represented his only hope of redemption and survival in LA.

"What a dump," opined Drea in her best Bette Davis voice.

"It's alright," James said defensively.

He walked behind the bar and just before he got to the cashier's window from the inside, he saw a pair of Technics turntables and his imagination took flight. "I just have to get the right artists and it can work here."

"I grew up in LA and believe me, most kids have barely heard of Silver Lake, let alone know how to get here."

"Yeah, I know, but at least it's on Sunset. I mean, all you have to do is head east, right?"

He walked to the far end of the room. There was a tiny dressing room cut into the wall with a tatty curtain on a rail for "privacy."

Behind the bar was a small, mildewy office, its only contents an old wooden desk and two chairs. He walked behind the bar to the DJ setup. The two turntables were the only new-looking items in the place, along with a mike. He couldn't resist flipping it on. He yelled, "Oi! Oi! Oi!" and heard his reverbed voice bounce off the walls in a very satisfying way. He walked back out front to where Drea stood.

He reached for the payphone on the wall. "Let's take a cab back. Want to go eat at Barney's Beanery before the Selecter show at the Whisky? I want to make sure we get there in time for Geno Washington's opening set..."

An hour later, he was tearing into pork chops at Barney's bar solo as Drea had gone home to change. As he reached for his Scotch, he realized Joe Strummer was sitting next to him.

"You English, right?" asked the Clash singer.

"Yeah. I live here now, though."

"How'd that happen?"

"Bit of a long story but I gotta say, at the risk of sounding corny, the Clash inspired me to get up and do something with my life, ya know?"

Strummer nodded. "I'm going up to see the Selecter and Geno Washington at the Whisky."

"Yeah, me too."

James pulled out a couple of Black Bombers, throwing one back along with the rest of his Scotch and offering the other cap of time-released speed to Strummer.

"Thanks, don't mind if I do."

They got their respective checks and took the fairly short walk up from Santa Monica Boulevard.

"What are you doing here?" asked the singer.

"About to start a ska and soul club. Listen, it was genius that Lee Dorsey played with you at the Santa Monica Civic. How did you manage to get him to do that?"

Without a trace of sarcasm, Strummer said, "We asked him."

Club owner Mario, who had always acted like a kindly uncle or perhaps more appropriately godfather to James, stood outside the Whisky as they crossed Sunset. The house had turned over from the early show, which would have been more industry dominated, and a steady stream of kids was entering for the eleven thirty show.

The Specials' performances earlier in the year had clearly left an impression. Inside, it was shoulder to shoulder. At one of the few booths against the back wall that faced the stage, the other members of the Clash held court.

James was slightly disappointed to see champagne bottles on ice. *Punk's not dead, right? Everything really is changing.*

Strummer apparently felt the same and suggested they stand closer to the stage. They went up a couple of steps on the staircase that led to the upstairs bar and balcony to get a better view.

Geno Washington's band, who looked like vaguely hippyish rockers, started plugging in their instruments, not a good sign to James. But when the towering, shaved-headed Geno Washington strode on stage and let rip, his fears were largely dispelled. The audience mostly only knew who he was from the recent Dexys Midnight Runners homage to him. But the mix of originals and soul covers were well received and the man could still deliver big-time.

During the last song, an oversized biker security guy coming down from the balcony yelled "get off the stairs" to Strummer and gave him a shove to emphasize, sending the singer stumbling into James. As pissed off as this made James, he liked that Strummer didn't have a "do you know who I am?" moment. They headed up to the balcony bar after the set for more Scotch. The whizz was starting to kick in beautifully.

"Shall we go and say hello to Mr. Washington?" asked Strummer.

The entrance to the Whisky's backstage was at the end of the balcony and the on-guard biker, unlike the jackass on the stairs, noticed the stickers Mario had given them and wordlessly stood aside.

A corridor led to several dressing rooms. Geno's was open and the sweating soul man was sitting topless and smiling, his bandmates kidding around.

He and Strummer hugged, although James couldn't quite tell if they'd met before. It was established that Geno was living in Los Angeles with his longtime wife Frenchie.

Emboldened by Strummers's simple "we asked him" Lee Dorsey comment, not to mention the dazzling speed buzz, James said, "So Geno, I'm starting a soul and ska club down the 'uvva end of Sunset. Any chance I could talk you into playing?"

"Well, we hadn't planned on playing many gigs. I'm finishing up a course in hypnotism."

"Mate, it would be a tragic waste if you don't play more shows."

Geno smiled. "Well, Frenchie here's in charge of all that. Why don't you give us your number and maybe we can talk about it?"

James exchanged numbers with the tall blonde.

Joe said, "Write your name down on something for me. We're gonna do a surprise show at the Roxy Sunday. I'll put you on the list."

They left the band to unwind and saw the Selecter members heading down the staircase that led directly onto the stage. They could feel the adrenaline pulsing from the band.

"Best go and find my band, too, James. Want to come?"

"Thanks, Joe. I was supposed to meet a girl here. I should have a look for her."

He couldn't spot Drea as he gazed down from the balcony. As the band blazed into "Too Much Pressure," he maneuvered his way close to the stage, awash in the amphetamine energy and dreams of what his club could become. *Putting bands like this in that joint and revving the crowd all night with the right records they'd never hear on the radio will rule. That fucking Oriental Nights name, though. Wait. What if we just shorten it to the initials O.N. and put Klub on the end like in the Specials' song "Night Klub"? Fuck, that's it.*

It was about 1:15 a.m. as he filed out with the rest of the punters. Just enough time to walk down the block to the Corner Pocket before the 2:00 a.m. closing. Dwight Twilley's "I'm on Fire" was playing as he walked into the dimly lit beer bar. The handful of pool tables were occupied by the usual assortment of beautiful and not-so-beautiful losers. He grabbed a stool at the tiny bar at the far end of the room to enjoy the ice-cold draft beer in a thin, chilled glass.

"What are you looking so happy about?" asked the long-suffering barman Jerry.

"Fuck, mate, didn't realize I did. Just dreaming like everyone else, I s'pose."

18

As he drank a second beer, he did allow the dream to take hold. The show had made him dead sure the club could work. *Spinning the right records with bands like that will be genius.* He knew he had to move on from everything to do with Real Records and the Confederacy band plane crash as quickly as possible. For a split second, he saw backup singer Sue Ann walking toward the plane that night but downing the rest of the beer chased the vision away. He had one more to make sure she didn't come right back and put a quarter on the nearest pool table, figuring that would be a good distraction too.

The deal here was your quarter would put you up against whoever won the current game.

That turned out to be a stocky Irishman from Belfast who looked a few years older and sounded as if he'd been drinking at an even faster pace than James that night. They both shot pretty well considering the inebriation levels. James had grown up playing on full-size snooker tables and had a tendency to strike the ball too hard for the smaller pool tables and lost this round. They had a very amiable conversation between shots as they shared a lot of musical taste but got into a heated debate about a Van Morrison song lyric. Now, as a rule, James would never back down on such matters, but something about the guy's certitude gave him pause.

He headed back onto the Strip as the bar was closing, wondering if the guy had actually been Van Morrison and if Norman, the name he'd introduced himself with, was for anonymity.

A stunning vintage red Cadillac convertible with the top down rolled by, occupied by the Clash.

Now if that's not a good omen, what is?

He walked south and turned left onto Fountain. But as he got nearer his beautiful turreted deco apartment building, he felt the presence of a white Ford Crown Victoria crawling along beside him. As he walked a little more swiftly up the walkway, it stopped and two heavyset guys in worn-looking suits jumped out and moved quickly to either side of him.

"How's it going, killer?"

"It's going fucking great, thanks, and I think Jerry Lee Lewis already copyrighted that nickname, by the way."

"Well, that's not good, is it, Fred?" said the taller of the two sheriff's department homicide detectives whose worn suit was more mid-seventies leisure meets disco compared to the other's fifties Joe Friday *Dragnet* rip-off. He was otherwise distinguished from his partner by the heavy Southern twang, longer hair, and newly capped teeth, whereas the other, older lawman was still regulation crew cut and badly in need of dental help.

"No, Johnny, it's not. We don't like killers happy and free in our neighborhood. Why don't we all go inside and see what we can do about this sorry state of affairs?"

"Sorry, boys. It's past my bedtime. Some other time, maybe."

Johnny stood crowding James until his back almost touched his front door. "Now, that's the wrong attitude, Dual. When we happened to spot you just now, it reminded us we were overdue to spend some quality time together. Last time you visited our place, and it's very rude of you not to return the invitation."

"Yeah, unforgivable, I'm sure. Your interview rooms and interrogation techniques are so charming. Where are my manners?"

Fred stepped in now, so close that James could smell the stale breath that went along with the bad teeth and somewhat tarnished his clean-cut *Dragnet* vibe.

"Listen, you skinny limey punk. The FBI may have written you off as a suspect but we flat out don't like your attitude or having you in West Hollywood, so we are going to keep digging to find a way to pin this on you, guilty or otherwise. We know your act. You've got a big mouth and sooner or later you'll let something slip about that crash to some broad or other when you've had one too many. Meantime, maybe we will become your new best friends. We'll come visit. Take you out for breakfast and shit when our shift starts at five a.m. You'll like that. Or just drop by, like now, for a nightcap. It's going to be great."

He put his meaty hand against James's chest and shoved him hard into the door. "Nighty night for now."

CHAPTER 4

JAMES WOKE UP KNOWING he had to get some artists booked for the club, which he'd agreed to have open within a month. He loved his 1931-built, courtyard-style, one-bedroom, second-floor apartment with its turret bedroom window, deco fixtures, and thick white adobe walls that allowed him to play his music at ferocious volume without ever hearing from his neighbors. Fountain Avenue was expensive, though, and without the Real Records dollars going into his bank account twice a month, he needed to make money sharpish. Thank fuck Real had got him a green card.

He did get hold of recently met pal Perry Watts-Russell, who managed the only LA ska band, the Boxboys, and got them booked before Drea called.

"Hey, honey. I'm outside the punk apartments. I'm scoring some dope and just heard there's a party later at Errol Flynn's old place on Runyon Canyon. Wanna go?"

Despite having been here a while, James was always happily nonplussed on hearing another Hollywood icon's home was now the playground of punks, dopers, and other assorted miscreants.

"Of course. Want me to get a cab and come pick you up in a few hours?"

"Okay. Don't forget, 'kay? I have no desire to spend the night here and catch God knows what."

He grinned and went back to booking. He got hold of Patrick Barrow, who had a reggae band James liked, the Babylon Warriors. There was some back and forth as they usually got a guarantee and James was only doing percentages of the ticket sales, but the affable bass player agreed to give it a try.

He called Yellow Cab and was duly picked up fifteen minutes later. He detoured the driver via Bogie's Liquor at Melrose and Vine, knowing they were the only place he could be sure would have a bottle of Bell's Scotch. He hopped out and his confidence in the run-down but well-stocked spot was duly rewarded with a fifth of Bell's. He grabbed a bottle of Kamchatka Vodka for Drea, along with a couple of packs of Gitanes, figuring it was likely to be an all-night affair.

The punk apartments, or the Canterbury as it was formally named, was a four-story building located at Cherokee and Yucca just north of Hollywood Boulevard. To call it a run-down shithole would be a gross understatement, but its extremely low rent and proximity to the Masque punk club had made it perfect for a lot of the LA punks, most of whom had bands. James left the booze in the cab by way of deposit while he went in to find her.

The vile, undefinable smell hit him as soon as he pushed through the double doors. He saw Alice Bag and Phranc, leaning against the stairwell, deep in conversation. He walked up the soggy carpeted stairs as music crackled out of various rooms. He pushed the half-open door of Margo Olavarria's room and the odds-on favorite came in as he saw Drea draped, nodding, across a saggy brown couch also inhabited by Bags man Terry Graham and a gesticulating Darby Crash, lead singer of the notorious Germs.

"Oi, oi, Darby, you alright?" he interrupted, instantly repelled by the smack-proffering creep kneeling on the floor in front of the Germs singer.

"Yeah, I'm back from London."

"I can fucking tell that, Darby. Nice mohawk. I know your heart's in the right place, but you do know every wanker in Chelsea's got one and is selling pictures to tourists, right?"

The singer smiled wanly.

James looked at Drea, torn. Their friendship was based on no rules whatsoever except utter loyalty, so despite his heroin hatred he left the subject alone. He'd first met her at the Rainbow Bar and Grill on the Sunset Strip. They'd bonded over a similar musical teen transition from the Velvet Underground to the transcendent glam of Bowie and Roxy Music to punk, along with a mutual love of 1940s crime novels and films. She'd taken him home with her but it had never occurred to either of them to put any relationship label or rules of fidelity in place. She had a fearless "fuck you," streetwise attitude that, when meshed with his relentless "bullshit detector," frequently caused trouble for those who crossed their path.

"Cab's outside. Wanna get out of here?"

"Why don't we have a drink here first?" she asked.

"I got you sorted in the cab."

She grinned, her black hair falling across half her face like a young Gloria Swanson.

"Let's get the fuck out of here then."

"Are you going to that party? Can I catch a ride?" asked Darby.

They threaded their way out through the tangle of entwined bodies, beer cans, empty booze bottles, and slippery flooring.

Drea directed the cab driver west on Sunset and up Fuller to Runyon Canyon. Darby was barely in the back seat of the cab before he half nodded out. A new moon hung over the eerie hills and for a while they could only hear coyote yips. But then the sound of Joy Division's "She's Lost Control" became apparent.

The cab pulled up outside ornate double iron gates that were hanging open, where it looked as if someone had hacksawed the padlock and chain.

They exited the cab, bottles in hand. There were a series of burnt-out stone cottages near a very deep but empty movie-star-size swimming pool. A crowd of people was drinking in the pool, which was also where a turntable and big speakers—aided by the acoustics—boomed Ian Curtis's voice into the night.

"I can't wait for the Joy Division show at the Starwood," said Drea.

"Yeah, me an' all," said James. "What are you gonna do now you're back?" he asked Darby.

"Start a new band. No one will book the Germs 'cause of our crowd violence," the singer lamented.

"You're well optimistic if you think they'll book you at all. Maybe you should play places like this."

"Is it true you're starting a club, James?"

"Yeah. I'm gonna do ska and soul, though. Outside of you lot and the Clash, I'm getting bored with punk."

"What the fuck about us?" A grinning Margo Olavarria, punk soul of the Go-Go's—hands in jeans, elbows out, and, to James, an absolute kindred spirit—was clearly ready to have at it.

"You still a punk band?" he teased. "Anyway, I hear you are going to tour with Madness in England and maybe the Specials. Sounds like we're headed in the same direction."

"Yeah, I heard you're doing a club. About time. We might do you a favor."

He handed her the bottle of Bell's. "It's all changing, Margo, but I think it's gonna be good for us. Anyway, what are you doing here? There's a scene at your place."

She shrugged. "The scene there's changing too, and it feels like some people aren't going to make it out of the seventies. I don't know if I like the changes in my band either since Elissa left, but fuck it." She took a long hit on the fifth of Scotch.

"It'll be alright. They will love you in England and you like London, right? Going away will open everything up. The hardcore thing here is going to be so boring too."

She grinned. "Make sure you cause double trouble to make up for my absence."

A stunning statuesque woman with a towering afro strode by, headed toward a wooden pergola up above them.

"That's Marsha Hunt. You should get her," said Drea.

"Are you sure? What would she be doing here? Wait, I think it is. What shall I say to her?"

Drea grabbed his arm and marched them up the steep incline.

The singer, dressed in matching white thigh-length boots, miniskirt, and a bikini-like top with strings all along the sleeves, was silhouetted against the desolate skyline.

"Hey, my friend James is starting a soul and ska club on Sunset, and you need to play there."

"Does your friend do all your talking for you?" said the artist most knew by her chilling rendition of "Walk on Gilded Splinters."

"I mostly hold my own. Would you be interested? I'm gonna play great vintage soul and ska, mixed with the 2 Tone bands,"

"You think I'm vintage, honey?"

"Um, no. 'Iconic' would be a better word. Seriously, you would be perfect."

"Well, I am working on some new songs while I'm here. It might make sense. I'd need to have plenty of rehearsal time. Do you have a great sound system? There'd best be excellent monitors. I need to hear myself, you understand? Are you opening on the Strip?"

James figured the complete absence of everything she wanted could be worked out along the way.

"Your first diva, huh?" said Drea as they descended back into the increasingly out-of-control crowd below.

CHAPTER 5

THE WEEKS LEADING UP to the opening blazed by in a haze of activity. Old mates the Adaptors understood his soul band notion and recruited East LA horn players from Los Lobos to "adapt" themselves into a soul review.

James got hold of his best friend in London, Ross, and somehow convinced him to air freight all his old Stax records, along with the ska and bluebeat records he'd grown up with but left at the East End of London house they had shared.

Most of it dated to the mid to late 1960s, by which time London's Jamaican population had quickly grown to 200,000 in a decade—luckily for kids like James, who would never have been exposed to the music otherwise. Adopted first by the mods and then skinheads, both Jamaican ska and later bluebeat were heavily influenced by American Southern soul, and he was sure they would all work together on the dance floor. Jerry Dammers's new 2 Tone label, with its racially unifying punky ska releases from England, would be the core, though: It was what would keep everything looking forward instead of being nostalgic.

James had originally come to LA for a holiday but since Terry Harper hired him to an A&R position at Real Records, he had never been back.

For two weeks, James and the band drank until the bars closed at 2:00 a.m. and then posted flyers on the walls of the Whisky and other clubs, knowing full well they'd be torn off the next night by pissed-off club owners. But hopefully word would get around. They also hit every telegraph pole along Hollywood Boulevard, Sunset Boulevard, Santa Monica Boulevard, and Melrose Avenue, concentrating most heavily on the blocks where clubs, record shops, or boutiques were located. By the time May 17 rolled round, he was quietly confident people would show up.

He loaded all the records he wanted for the night into a milk crate and he and Drea rode a Yellow Cab east to 3037 Sunset.

He grinned, hearing the nine-piece band sound-checking as they walked in. Drea had agreed to work the ticket window until he could afford to pay someone, and he had hired a neighborhood kid, Alberto, to check IDs and make sure no one snuck in without paying. They opened the door at eight. He played mostly dub reggae, while waiting nervously to see whether anyone would show up beyond the band's guest-listed friends, who trickled in for the next hour. By nine, Drea was scrambling to make change as a line formed outside.

He dropped the Specials' "Message to You Rudy" and saw the first group of kids hit the dance floor. He kept them there with a steady flow: the Upsetters' "Return of Django," Althea & Donna's "Uptown Top Ranking," Harry J & the All Stars' "The Liquidator," Otis Redding's "I Can't Turn You Loose." By the time he got ready to announce the Adaptors and their Low Rider Horns' first set an hour later, the joint was packed with a fun mix of punters, many obviously 2 Tone inspired—the porkpie hats, etc., a dead giveaway. Another good sign was the bar moving beers faster than light. The band delivered just like a soul band should.

The sweaty, giddy crowd didn't get a break. They were hit with the English Beat's "Twist & Crawl" before they could catch a breath. And so it continued. As 2:00 a.m. loomed, no one was leaving. Finally, James figured out where the main lights were, put on the Specials' "You're Wondering Now," the lyrics encouraging a begrudging acceptance that LA closes too early. He heard a Jamaican accent and spotted a girl, who could have been Millie Small if this was 1964 and

27

"My Boy Lollipop" had just hit shelves, exiting with some friends through the narrow entrance.

He cashed out and gave the band their cut of the door before they all got into the serious celebrating of a job well done.

When he got home, though, there was a message on his machine from Norman saying that the Joy Division show they had tickets for had been canceled because singer Ian Curtis had committed suicide in Manchester the day before they left for America.

Fuck, just as he would have seen other possibilities, James thought. *So close.* He thought about how many concerned friends in London had told him he'd be gone soon if he kept up his current lifestyle. As much as he loved Manchester and London, there truly seemed no hope there right now, and despite everything, Los Angeles felt like the place where you could create your own reality. He knew he had to make this club work like his life depended on it, 'cause it probably did.

CHAPTER 6

It was fucking rama lama ding dong for the next few months.

Geno Washington rolled in and conjured up all his soul power, which he needed while dragging his long-haired hippy band where he needed them to be, but it worked.

James heard English accents too now. He instantly liked Louise and Kalle, with their Clash-inspired clothes and experience taking the same cheap Freddie Laker flight to LA he had. Lou soon took over from a keen-to-retire Drea at the ticket window, and her boyfriend worked the door here and there.

There was at least twice the legal capacity most nights and kids crawling up the walls, looking for dance space. Around this time *LA Weekly* music editor Bill Bentley dubbed the joint "The House of Sweat" in his preview of the first LA show by ace ska band the X-Streams.

As opposed to the increased violence and open misogyny in the burgeoning hardcore scene, there was no fighting on the dance floor, shared by Jamaicans, South Central kids, art punks, sharp-dressed Asian American girls, and mod kids on scooters from Orange County, along with a growing number of neighborhood Latino kids united by the vinyl they can't hear on the radio—or anywhere else in LA, for that matter.

Marsha Hunt put James through his paces with an array of needs but absolutely delivered come the night, climaxing with a shiver-inducing rendition of "Walk on Gilded Splinters."

The night LA's only ska band, the Boxboys, played, it was so hot that the crowd rotated out onto the street before diving back in for more. James loved it—the fire department, not so much. But he escaped with a warning.

He walked in late afternoon for sound check the day the Babylon Warriors were booked to see a guy who looked like a stockier version of fifties Latino rock and roller Ritchie Valens, his black hair Brylcreemed into a widow's peak, sporting a sharp, gray-flecked heavy cotton suit and gray loafers with no socks, sitting at the bar of the otherwise empty club, drinking a beer he had presumably helped himself to.

"Can I 'elp you?"

"Join me, Mr. Dual." He put a business card on the bar as James acquiesced. It read Detective Sergeant Franc Mata, LAPD Rampart Division.

Fuck.

"Heard you had a visit from the fire department last weekend."

"Yeah. What of it?"

"I think you are going to get to know those guys really well if you keep going on the way you are. Still, that's your worry, not mine."

"And what's your worry?"

"That I'm going to have to visit this shithole again, if you keep serving underage kids."

Unlike London, where there were no IDs and if you looked sort of old enough, you were set, LA had a strict twenty-one-year-old age limit, even if you were only serving beer and wine.

James wanted that teenage energy, though, so he turned a complete blind eye to the proliferation of fake IDs.

"Look, my doorman checks IDs. How am I supposed to tell? I've never been a good judge of age."

"You'd best wise up if you want to stay open."

"Look at it this way: we are doing you lot a favor keeping the kids off the streets.

"There's no violence going on in here. Just dancing. Jesus, the girl who sells the tickets went to the liquor store on the corner to get some

30

change and had to duck from bullets hitting the neon sign on top. She was well shaken up, I can tell you. Haven't you got more important things to handle?"

"Listen, Dual. I'm presuming there's drugs being consumed and maybe actively sold."

James knew LA had been way more about Quaaludes than speed, the clear drug of choice for the club's regulars, so kept pushing his luck. "What—you mean like Quaaludes and shit? I've never seen anyone falling on downers here."

"You are wide open. You may have skated on that plane crash beef, and that case isn't on my turf, but keep it squeaky clean here. Play by our rules or you'll learn way more about Rampart than you can handle."

It didn't exactly help matters that the Babylon Warriors and entourage arrived on a cloud of smoke as the cop exited. He wondered whether Mata wanted a payoff.

The band was a split of Belizean and Jamaican guys who were rock solid and authentic, with a young lead singer with charisma to burn. They tore it up for the packed-out crowd. James sat on a stool at the bar, still pensive, when the Millie Small look-alike from opening night strode effortlessly through the dense dance floor.

"This your place, right?"

"At the moment, yes."

She grinned. "These guys are alright but you need more ska bands."

His turn to grin. "Maybe."

"This is your lucky day, because I have one."

He looked at her a bit more closely. She had the same poise and infectious grin as the singer of 1964's "My Boy Lollipop" fame but was likely still too young to be legally in the club. She wore half-inch black braces over a crisp white shirt and what looked like black Levi's STA-PREST—much like his own, in fact. A black porkpie hat was tilted slightly to the left.

"Yeah?"

31

She took the hat off and pulled a cassette tape from behind the hat band. "Here's a rehearsal tape. We haven't played out yet, but if you ask nicely, we could do our first gig here."

"You think you are ready for all this?" He swept an arm out at the mayhem on the dance floor.

"The question should be, can they handle us? We'll put these wannabe rude boys through their paces, that's for damn sure."

He took the cassette from her, looking at the handwritten label. "Alright, I'll have a listen. Top Ranking, huh?"

"I'm Loraine Sulley. My number's on there."

Lenny, the Yellow Cab driver he now had a standing 2:00 a.m. pick-up arrangement with, leaned on the horn as the last strains of "You're Wondering Now" ended the night as usual.

"Oi, Lenny, bang this tape on while we ride home, eh?"

The quiet, melancholy tough guy, with a black crew cut, reminded James of Travis Bickle in *Taxi Driver*, but he had refrained from mentioning it despite how happy the similarity made him.

The drive west took them through a gradual economic climb of neighborhoods. Top Ranking were raw as fuck and a little sloppy here and there, but he knew he was gonna book them.

He was looking forward to a drink to start winding down with as they dropped south from Sunset to Fountain. But as he exited the cab and reached for his crate of records, he saw a light on in his bedroom window. *For fuck's sake, not more cops.* He didn't carry a gun despite Selva's urging but wished he had something right now.

He handed Lenny some bills. "Do me a favor, Lenny, and stay put for a minute. I may have unwanted visitors. I don't see a Crown Vic but make sure I don't get dragged off by the law, okay?"

"Sure, Jimmy."

He carried the crate up to his front door and quietly opened it. He didn't turn on the downstairs lights and made his way up the circular stairs.

His bedroom door was half open. He kicked it the rest of the way. The deco lamp on the bedside table was on low.

A half-undressed woman was curled face down. The bullet belt and high boots on the floor let him exhale. He put his hand gently on her shoulder.

"Drea, you okay? I haven't seen you for weeks."

She stirred and ran her fingers across her lips. "Yeah, just about, honey. I had a near miss. My parents sicced some crazy rehab people on me last month. They grabbed me outside my place and threw me in some semi hospital van. Drove me out to Orange County and checked me in. It was like a prison camp. No dope or booze, and I was getting force-fed vile beef with mashed potatoes and shit."

"Are you serious?" he said incredulously.

"Fuck yeah. I think my mother's agent was behind it. Pretty sure my dad wouldn't pull something like this."

"How'd you escape?"

"I was in the dorm room last night, when they put the lights out—at ten, if you can believe that—and I saw my chance to escape. The usual door guard was out sick so I climbed out the window onto a fire escape. I shimmied up the surrounding wall but they actually had barbed wire up there."

She sat up now, and he could see her grazed knees and cut hands.

"It took four hitched rides and twenty-four hours, but I finally got to Hollywood a couple of hours ago. I was scared to go to my place. My parents don't have your address, so this seemed to be the best bet."

He went downstairs, letting Lenny know it was okay to bail and made two Bell's Scotch and waters.

He unlaced his officer's boots and lay next to her.

"There's something else I've got to tell you that happened the night before those fuckers kidnapped me. I was outside the Rainbow, waiting for a cab, and two plainclothes cops tell me they want to talk to me. Said they'd drive me home. Like it wasn't a choice, ya know?"

"Fuck me. Did one have a heavy Southern accent and the other look like he was from one of those old TV cop shows your dad was in?"

"Yep. When they pulled up outside my place without me needing to tell them my address, it gave me the creeps, and then they started in. Told me I'm keeping some dangerous company and that they need my help to get you off the streets for the benefit of all. I told them to basically fuck off, at which point the Southern one, who was in the front passenger seat, reached back, put his closed fist against my chest, and opened his palm, which dropped a gram or so of smack in my lap. Said Sybil Brand Women's Prison would be rough for a pretty little girl like me. Told me the inmates have found some very unusual uses for broom handles. I probably wouldn't survive. Not to mention that the sheriffs who run the place like to do the odd sleepover with the young ones like me. Said he might even stop by for a sample himself. I started screaming at him that I didn't know anything and even if I did, I wouldn't tell a piece of shit like him. But I was scared as hell. The old one said they'd give me a chance to get you talking and that I'd be seeing them again soon."

"Those motherfuckers. Between the bent sheriffs and the rehab nuts, I think it's time you took a bit of a London Calling holiday. Know what I mean? I can sort you a place to hide out for a bit."

She grinned. "Like Chas at Turner's Notting Hill basement place in 'Performance'?"

"Well, hopefully I can make sure Ross looks after you better than Mick Jagger did James Fox in that film so you don't get found."

CHAPTER 7

THE NIGHT OF TOP Ranking's show, James saw *LA Weekly* music editor Bill Bentley in a line that ran around the block.

"Oi, Bill. You better come in with me. I think that 'Scoring the Clubs' preview you wrote may have had a bit to do with the queue, so hardly seems fair you get stuck out here on account of it. By the way, I like you nicknaming us 'The House of Sweat.'"

"I'm lucky to be here at all." The soulful, skinny Austin native grinned. "I was a bit the worse for wear after Geno Washington's show. Top Jimmy and Carlos Guitarlos from the Rhythm Pigs dropped me on my damn head while they were carrying me to the car. Instead of taking me to the hospital—which no one had money for—they put me on Jimmy's couch. I came to two days later."

"You kidding me? Fucking hell, mate. Let's get you sorted on a barstool before the doors open."

The crowd poured in in a hurry. This wasn't a night to ease in with dub, so he dropped the Specials' "Too Much Too Young" and made a quick visit to the curtained, what passed for a dressing room, space. Loraine and the band, whom he'd barely met, looked a little tense. They were a multiracial mix and all looked as if they were still in their teens, except for the two older horn players.

"You alright, then? I'll get the crowd well revved up and you go on for the first set in an hour, okay? If you have a song you wanna hear right before, tell me now, and it can be a cue before I announce you."

"What do you think, James? Want to put me in a box and play 'On My Radio' by the Selecter? Maybe 'My Boy Lollipop' like that Millie Small girl you think I look like?"

"Nervous, are you, girl?" he said teasingly. "Don't take it out on me. You asked for this. Have a think about it."

He walked behind the bar, dodging the already busy bartender, and headed toward the turntables, slipping on the Pioneers' "Long Shot Kick De Bucket" just in time. He wasn't worried about Loraine as every instinct told him that, nervous or not, she'd back up her big talk. He liked her and the playfully combative tone that had been set for their working relationship. She'd been right that first night: he did need more ska bands to keep things fresh too, so they both had a lot riding on the show.

He saw another recently met friend, *LA Times* Pop Eye columnist Patrick Goldstein, who stood by Bill Bentley at the bar, along with a towering, shaved-headed guy in a gray silk designer suit, who dwarfed the six-foot-plus writer.

"Hey, James," Patrick yelled. "Come over once the band's on. I brought someone to meet you."

Loraine hadn't picked a song by nine, so he put on the Selecter's "Too Much Pressure" to fuck with her just a bit.

She stuck her head out of the dressing room and flipped him a playful V-sign.

He got on the mike attached to his turntables and started talking over the record to the packed crowd. "Oi! Oi! I'm excited to introduce…for the first time…Top Ranking."

The band was nervously plugging in, stray bits of feedback echoing. Loraine bounced on the spot like a fighter, throwing little jabs.

"I hope you lot are ready to dance. They told me they are going to put you through your damn paces, right, Loraine?"

He knew it was a bit risky to give her such a provocative introduction, but she and the band responded, blazing into amped-up ska right out of the gate. They still weren't super tight but the overall sound and especially the horn players held it together while Loraine went about her business. She started out prowling around the stage, singing her passionate, raw, social lyrics, dropping to her haunches here and there, singing right into a kid's face to emphasize her point. Six songs in, she was prancing back and forth across the stage, pretty much owning the crowd.

James relaxed and went out to the front of the bar where Patrick introduced him to his guest.

"This is Tony Marshall. In case you didn't know, he discovered Bob Marley. I was talking to him about the *Uprising* record and thought you'd get a kick out of meeting each other."

James's hand disappeared into Marshall's massive right hand as they shook. "I like your joint. Almost feels like I'm in Kingston," said the giant of a man.

James assumed the guy was Jamaican, but was there a Southern US tone in there too? "Thanks. An honor to have you here. I've been playing the new record a lot."

"Great. There might be some things we can do together. Bob's not going to do any surprise small club shows but I'm also managing Bunny Wailer. We should get together while I'm here. How about I take you to lunch next Tuesday?"

"Brilliant."

"What's the story with your little girl here? She's not bad."

"Well, she's not my little girl, or probably anyone else's, for that matter. But Top Ranking are just starting out."

"Interesting."

James noticed kids from the audience were jumping on stage, hoping to skank with Loraine. "Excuse me, Tony. I need to deal with this."

"I understand. I have a club in New York, although I don't believe anyone ever tried to jump on my stage."

Looking at the imposing guy, James didn't imagine they would either.

He got back to the turntables and, when the band finished the song, yelled over the mike. "Anyone who isn't playing an instrument, get off the fucking stage, now!"

Repeating that a few times had the desired effect and the band finished the set with the stage mostly to themselves.

CHAPTER 8

48 Margaret Street, London W1.

DESPITE ACTING HER USUAL nonchalant self, Drea was inwardly jazzed to finally get to notorious private rock and roll watering hole the Speakeasy. She'd been bugging James's best friend Ross to go ever since she'd arrived in London. It was around 11:30 p.m. and Dr. Feelgood's "Keep It Out Of Sight" played as Ross pulled his dark-blue, windowless van into a parking spot just across the narrow street. They'd finished a bottle of gin with his housemate Jeni before leaving the east London house.

It hadn't been so bad staying there. Ross was a fun English rock and roller and a good guy, even if he did really remind her of tennis player Björn Borg. There didn't seem to be much to do where they lived but they drank a lot and got to consume a pleasing variety of drugs, including the wonderful local amphetamine sulfate they'd snorted on the way out.

None of this crowd took heroin, though, and she wondered if that was partly why James had thought of her going to London. He never said anything, but she could tell he didn't approve of the heroin.

The three of them walked through the inconspicuous, narrow doorway and down a dimly lit set of stairs and turned left into a small entryway. There was a closed door to the left and a booth where four long black-haired rock and rollers were trying to talk their way in.

"Jim, you got to let us in. We're the Heavy Metal Kids, for fuck's sake."

"Gary, you lot are well overdue with your membership fees. This is the last time, alright?" said the club's longtime, long-suffering manager with a slight upward head turn.

Drea looked up to where an array of bounced checks adorned the wall, most of which featured well-known musician's names. Ross handed Jim his membership card, along with some pound notes. "Two guests tonight, okay, Jim?"

The manager looked up at the stunningly beautiful blonde, cropped-haired, Bowiesque Jeni, and ever dangerous-looking Drea and nodded.

Jeni turned to Drea. "Fancy pulling a couple of cute guys for the night?"

They entered a crowded narrow area. The Commodores' "Machine Gun" played.

There was a horseshoe bar on the left. Ahead of them was a set of double saloon-style swing doors that Jeni told Drea led to the restaurant. They spotted three seats at the far side of the bar and beelined for them, easing their way through a mix of trendily dressed Chelsea girl types, a few punks, and various rock and rollers, most of whom Drea recognized immediately from one band or another.

The attractive, Biba makeup-adorned, round-eyed bartender obviously knew Ross and leaned herself across the bar to make sure she heard his order and, Drea thought, to make sure her good-looking host got an eyeful.

"Three Scotch and Cokes, please, Darla."

"Coming right up, baby. You do know there's a half-full bottle of Jack Daniels you bought last time you were here up on the bar?"

"Thanks, I'd forgotten. Maybe we'll get to it later."

Drea grinned. "Wishing you were in America, too, Ross?"

Darla returned with chunky glasses of Scotch and small bottles of Coke for them all. Drea poured Coke into the Scotch, creating what to her seemed an odd mix. "This reminds me. Is it true you poured a glass of Scotch and Coke all over Bryan Ferry the night Roxy Music's *For Your Pleasure* record came out?"

"Fucking hell. I wish James wouldn't tell that story. It makes me sound clumsy. I didn't exactly pour it over him. I was just making a point telling a story and my velvet jacket sleeve caught the glass but yeah, it did go all over him. I have to say, he was extremely gracious about it. He, of course, had a very tasty handmade suit from Alkasura on the Kings Road on as well."

Drea half turned, surveying the room. Lemmy, ex-bassist of Hawkwind and now fronting Motörhead, was playing Pong with a leather-jacketed young girl at the back of the bar. Across from the bar and parallel to the restaurant was a very small dance floor, with a low stage loaded with gear that looked ready for action later. Meantime, the DJ was keeping a small throng of dancers happy with Bowie's "John, I'm Only Dancing" straight into "The Jean Genie."

A loud yell of "Ross the boss" rang out and a hurtling diminutive ball of energy burst through the throng. Wearing a filthy, grease-ridden brown leather jacket and devastated Levi's to match, it looked like a mechanic who'd just rolled out from under a car but was in fact singer Stevie Marriott, one-time Small Faces' and more recently Humble Pie's front man.

"Where you been? Haven't seen you in ages," said Ross.

"Mostly in California. The Inland Revenue's after me for taxes in England that I thought my fucking manager had handled. I've been completely skint."

"Sorry, mate."

"It's alright. I've just been in New York, and me and Jerry Shirley are reforming Humble Pie. Got a bit of an advance from Atco."

"Well, that's good, but what about all the seventies money?"

"Lemme get a drink, and I'll tell you a mob story. Can the sorts keep their mouths shut?"

Jeni rolled her eyes. "Come on, Drea. Let's have a dance and find you a man for the night."

Drea, who, in truth, wasn't much for dancing but was ready to have some fun, followed in Jeni's wake. Jeni brushed off Sweet singer Brian Connolly's instant advance with "you're too old now."

They danced together to Bob and Earl's "Harlem Shuffle" before, out of the shadows near the stage, came drifting up a pair of tall, beautiful, gaunt, heavily made-up young goth guys.

"Now this is a bit more like it. Which one do you want, Drea?"

Drea liked this girl more and more. "Hmmm, close call. Maybe black eyes and blacker exploding hair?"

Jeni leaned in shoulder first to the one with the long-tailored coat and grasped his beautifully crafted three-inch silver crucifix. "You'd better make sure you don't lose this if you want to make it through the night, boy."

"Lady Marmalade" by LaBelle kicked in hard, as did Drea's Scotch and speed.

Back at the bar, Marriott took a long drink. "You won't fucking believe it, Ross, but I finally got away from that thieving cunt Don Arden but ended up with someone even worse in the States."

"Sorry, mate. I never met him but everyone's heard the stories about him hanging people out of his office windows when they go asking for their money, right?"

"See, I'd always known the American manager siphoned off Humble Pie money to fund promoting the *Frampton Comes Alive!* record. They spent a fortune of my money promoting that."

"We couldn't believe over here how big that record was in the States. Peter Frampton—remember Rave magazine called him 'The Face of '68.' Unbelievable. That seems like a million years ago," said Ross.

"So anyway. I keep going after the manager and finally I'm told to meet at the Ravenite Club in Little Italy in New York. I walk in there, right, and there's all these Gambino family mob guys—John Gotti, Paul Castellano, etc. They tell me I'm not getting any more fucking money and that I'd best shut the fuck up about it."

"Fucking hell. You serious?" said Ross.

"Serious as a fucking heart attack. Anyway, what are you going to do, right?" They ordered more drinks.

Marriott glanced across at the dance floor. "I see the sorts pulled the singer and guitar player from Vortex."

"Who?" asked Ross.

"You don't know them? They're getting big. *NME covers. Top of the Pops* appearance. Gothic post punk. I like their song 'Obliteration,' actually. Their turn to go try their luck in the States, I hear."

Rufus and Chaka Khan's "Tell Me Something Good" played as Drea and Jeni all but consummated their budding relationships on the dance floor.

"Listen, Roscoe, despite the 'charlie,' I'm actually hungry. Want to see if Luigi can take care of us?"

Ross was still feeling the whizz but acquiesced. He caught Jeni's eye and thumbed in the direction of the restaurant. They eased their way through and by the time the very tall, thin, angular maître d' Luigi walked up, Drea, Jeni, and the two goths had joined them.

The Italian touched a finger to the shock of combed-back black hair on his high forehead as he surveyed the two rows of booths that ran down the small area.

"Good evening, Mr. Marriott. Please come this way." He led them to the booth at the back that was on the side with the glass partition, giving them a nice view of the stage.

They all piled in. Luigi distributed menus and took orders without writing anything down.

Marriott ordered steak au poivre and Ross chicken Kiev with petit pois in their east London accents. Everyone else stuck with alcohol.

Hard to tell whether he was mocking their efforts but Luigi recapped: "One steak and chips, one chicken, chips, and peas, and six Scotch and Cokes."

Jeni introduced soft-spoken singer Guy, the one she had claimed, and guitar player Duncan, who had draped himself elegantly over Drea but was clearly fascinated to be in the presence of a big sixties and seventies star like Marriott.

"I hear you lot are off to the States soon," said Marriott.

"That's true. Next week, in fact. The record company set us up to play the 'Speak' tonight as a going-away party," said Guy in his well-spoken, "proper" English.

"I thought there was a lot of extra liggers in here tonight," said Ross. "Where are you playing in LA?" asked Drea.

"I'm pretty sure it's called the Roxy. I remember because I was told it's a lot more upmarket than the brilliant Covent Garden punk club was here," said Duncan.

"Oh, God, I loved that place. Do you remember how James would always drag you along, Ross?" said Jeni.

"Fucking hell. That first night when it opened, Generation X were playing and the toilets upstairs were leaking down on the stage from above. Horrible place."

"Oh, Ross," chided Jeni. "There were great shows, like the Boys."

"Talking of James and clubs. He's opened a brilliant one on Sunset in Silver Lake. Guy, Duncan—you should go when you are in LA," said Drea.

"That sounds good, Drea. LA's our last date. We are going to stay on for a while and meet some possible producers for the next record. Will you be going back soon? Maybe we could go together?" said Duncan.

"Um, my return is a little bit TBD."

Two rounds of drinks later, the food arrived and Guy and Duncan excused themselves to find the rest of the band.

Jeni whispered in Guy's ear as he rose. "Don't wear yourself out playing. You have a long night ahead of you."

He gave her an amused nod of acquiescence.

Jeni had the distinct sense that, unlike many lead singers, he didn't take himself too seriously and might be worth keeping for more than a one-night stand.

Vortex took the stage around 2:00 a.m. and impressed with a wall of apocalyptic guitar noise with Guy's vocals blending like another plaintive instrument. His charisma was undeniable to Drea, who thought this gig would be one people in the future would claim they were at. He and Duncan had an onstage rapport similar to David Bowie and Mick Ronson, but the singer was clearly the star. She wondered what had instantly attracted her to Duncan and decided that, just as if she'd been given the choice between Mick Jagger and

Keith Richards, Keef would win every time. Maybe living in a dream city like Los Angeles, she wanted earthier boys to balance things out a bit. One thing she was sure of was that the band would be instantly embraced in New York and Los Angeles.

The thick glass in the restaurant shielded the diners from the full sonic assault.

In the midst of the show, a leering Ginger Baker pawed Jeni from the booth across the aisle while making a lewd suggestion. She smiled and rose. Then she leaned toward him, apparently for a kiss, but slid her hand under his large plate of spaghetti and meatballs, which she carefully raised and pushed into his face. Marriott burst out laughing and his propensity for brawling deterred the angry drummer from doing anything beyond muttering "you fucking bitch" and heading off to clean up.

By the time Duncan and Guy extricated themselves from the variety of record label staff and the six of them stumbled up the stairs, it was almost 4:00 a.m. and Drea felt a little worse for wear. She couldn't quite believe that all the English seemed to drink even more than she did.

"Steve, where you staying? We'll drop you off," said Ross pushing in Stevie Wonder's Innervisions cassette.

"Nah, I got a suite at the Dorchester. It's well out of your way."

"Don't worry about it. You'll never get a cab at this time of night."

Drea, Jeni, Duncan, and Guy bundled into the back of the van in a tumble of drunken entwined limbs.

Ross blazed back down to Oxford Street and headed west to Mayfair. There was no traffic on the road, all pubs having closed five hours ago.

After the Dorchester drop, he headed east, flooring the van.

"Where exactly are we going?" asked Guy.

"To the Maybank Knocking Shop." Jeni laughed.

When she saw the look of horror on his face, she explained. "Don't worry, it's not really a brothel. That's just what our next-door neighbors call our house because there's so much late-night action."

Out of the darkness behind them came a siren and the flashing light of a police Rover.

"Fucking hell. I don't believe it. I'm so over the limit," said Ross.

Drea peered out of the back door's window at the Rover SD1 hurtling down The Mile End Road toward them, its V8 engine roaring in the otherwise quiet night. "Maybe they are on their way to a crime scene. They must be. Yay—they are going past us."

The optimism was short-lived as the Rover cut sharply in front of the van, forcing Ross to pull into the curb. The London cops had a different strategy than the LA ones she was used to, who would have stayed behind them.

Two uniformed officers approached the car, flashlight in hand. One came to the right-hand driver-side window.

"What do we have here, then? Out for a bit of late-night thieving, lad?" He leaned in a bit closer to Ross and theatrically recoiled. "Oh, and a lot of drinking, I'd say. Officer Ted, why don't you pop 'round the back and see what kind of swag our pretty long-haired friend has back there while I breathalyze him."

The younger of the two did as he was told and revealed the goth/glam/punk boy/girl drugged-up, fucked-up melee within.

Guy attempted to charm their way out of a likely arrest, well aware a drug bust could result in their US visas being revoked. "Terribly sorry to inconvenience you, Officer. Our record company insisted on us performing at an ungodly hour, so we had to prevail on our friends here to wait to take us home. My father, Lord Harding's, family estate is in Sawbridgeworth, Hertfordshire."

"So, what exactly have you been up to?" asked the older one of Ross.

"We are on our way home from the Speakeasy," said Ross quietly.

"Well, why didn't you say so, lad? We could have saved ourselves this unpleasantness. Now just make sure you go straight home. Drive safely and a little more slowly. Come on, Ted. Our business here is done."

As the Rover roared off into the night, there was silence in the van other than the trace of Stevie Wonder's "Too High" playing as the *Innervisions* cassette continued.

Drea finally broke the silence. "What the fuck just happened? There's enough dope in here to put us all away, not to mention you've got a least two bottles of liquor in you, Ross."

Ross shrugged. "That's London, innit? How do you think the Speak stays open until four a.m.? They pay the right lawmen. Got to admit, though, I didn't know that protection from police interference extended to this sort of thing these days. Maybe you dropping that your old man's a lord didn't hurt either, Guy."

CHAPTER 9

THE TEMPERATURES HAD BEEN creeping up gradually for weeks, along with a bonus solid layer of smog baking LA to a crisp, so when James walked downstairs to answer his door buzzer, the full effect of the one-hundred-degree heat hit him straight in the face. The towering figure of Tony Marshall in a sharp black suit, clearly making no sartorial concessions to the weather, blocked the direct glare of the sun.

"James, my man. So glad Patrick Goldstein was able to put us together. Come on, my car's just across the street. Let's go to lunch."

It was so hot James felt his neck burning just walking across Fountain to the presumably rented pale-blue Lincoln Continental Town Coupe. Its moonroof was closed but the glass made it even hotter inside the car than it was outside. Marshall powered up Holloway, onto Sunset. "I thought we'd go to Le Dome."

"Yeah, alright, Tony. Actually, though, you should've gone right at Sunset then." Marshall kept going up Sunset past the Whisky, the Roxy, and the Rainbow, making a U-turn at Doheny.

"Just have to make a quick stop here first." Marshall pulled over outside of a five-story glass office building. "Come up with me."

They took the elevator to the penthouse. It was very quiet up there. All off-white, with a set of hefty dark wooden doors that proclaimed in gold letters: "Accounting Firm of Marcott, Baines & Goldfarb."

Tony pulled open the right-hand door and ushered James in. There was a young, sophisticated woman with dark-red hair and a pale-blue Chanel suit sitting behind an ornate desk that matched the doors.

Tony strode up to within an inch of the desk. "Tony Marshall. I'm here to see Steve. I told him I was coming."

James couldn't tell whether she knew Marshall but she looked frightened as the giant of a man towered over her, way closer than he needed to be.

"Let me see if he is in."

"Tell him I'm here for my check."

She pressed a few buttons. James noticed that her hands shook. There was a brief exchange.

"I'm sorry, Mr. Marshall. Steve's not in."

"Stay here, James. I'll be right back. I forgot something from the car."

There was a tense, uncomfortable silence for several minutes as James and the girl looked at each other, both unsure what would happen. Then the double doors flew open again, led by an enormous baseball bat that crashed down the center of the desk, making a deep indentation while blasting the switchboard and everything else up into the air.

"Tell Steve to bring my money out." Marshall's unique Jamaican/American deep voice was quiet but unmistakably menacing.

The terrified woman raced through the door behind her desk.

"Sorry, James. This should just take a minute. I don't know about you but I'm getting hungry."

James surveyed the room, figuring either the LAPD would come blazing in the front door or some bodyguard would come out from the back, gun in hand. Instead, the receptionist returned, her shaking right hand proffering a check.

"So sorry, Mr. Marshall. I didn't realize Steve had left this for you."

"Right, baby. Not your fault. I see the ink is still wet." Tony chuckled.

◉◉◉

THE MAÎTRE D' AT Le Dome led them to an inside table to the right of the bar and sat them among an array of industry heavyweights, including Billy Wilder. Given the insane heat, James was happy not to be on the celebrity-dominated patio that Roger Moore had just been led to, despite the panoramic view. He felt oddly calm despite Marshall's violence, maybe because it had all felt surreal somehow, as if he were watching a film, and the giant man had acted throughout in an even, matter-of-fact manner, as if this were all perfectly normal. They ordered—James, soft shell crabs; Tony, the steamed pig knuckles.

The food came quickly, no doubt to help turn the tables during the busy lunch period. "So, James, I saw the big *LA Times* and *Herald Examiner* features on your club. I hear it's also a destination for all the hot young actors now."

"Yeah, the stories were great, but I don't pay much attention to whether actors come. I saw Larry Fishburne in line for the Boxboys the other night and I heard Jodie Foster likes to come, both of whom are cool by me."

"What do you mean? You have to look after celebrities. Don't their people ask to get them comped at least?"

"If anyone's getting in free, it's gonna be some broke kid scraping five bucks together and coming up a bit short. These record company people too. Fuck them. They all have expense accounts. They're paying for sure. Listen, my place will never be about that disco bullshit, velvet rope, VIP room, dress code, blah blah blah. Fuck all that shit."

Tony shook his head incredulously. "Unique way to set about things. Maybe you are onto something new I could be interested in. You know, I think I like you, Mr. Englishman. Perhaps it's time to take you to the next level." He chewed on the pig knuckle meditatively.

"How would you like it if I got Bunny Wailer to do a surprise show? He's got an album of Wailers songs out. It would help you get other Jamaican acts too."

"That would be cool. You know who I'd really like, though? Big Youth. Also, Clint Eastwood and General Saint."

"All possible. Big Youth's actually living in New York. I just saw him before I came out here to set up Bob's shows. Those other boys are signed to Greensleeves out of the UK. Not sure if that label is up to pulling together a US tour but maybe there's a way. Now, here's how you can help me. Your little girl could be a powerful figure like Bob, if I mold her the right way. In my hands she could go all the way. You need to deliver her to me, okay? She's got serious crossover potential."

So, here's what lunch is really about. James took a bite of the perfectly sautéed soft-shell crab. *The baseball bat episode a tasty appetizer designed to intimidate, huh?*

"I told you before, she's not my little girl, Tony. I'm reminding you because she's the one who will make a decision like that, not me, okay?"

Tony laughed his big, hearty laugh. "James, you underestimate yourself. You gave her her big chance. She'll listen to you and will trust your advice. I tell you what—just arrange a meeting for me and I'll do the rest. You don't even need to be there," said Marshall in the same precise, demanding, not-asking tone he'd used with the receptionist.

"I'll see what I can do."

"Excellent. I'll be at the Beverly Hills Hotel."

CHAPTER 10

DREA WOKE UP IN her tiny bunk as the battered Vortex tour bus navigated a tight bend just outside of Austin, Texas.

She yawned and wondered not for the first time why trekking across America in this cramped rig had seemed like such a good idea while lying in bed with Duncan back at Ross's place.

Admittedly, they had just had a pretty epic time and he had an easygoing, mischievous charm that made her like the idea of an extended period of hanging out together.

The long drives between cities was amplified by the band's insistence on being on Route 66 whenever possible. Rarely getting anything but day rooms in the shittiest Motel 6s, she felt perpetually skanky.

Still, there had been some fun moments. The band, particularly Duncan and Guy, were hell-bent on outdoing the Sex Pistols at offending as many people as possible across the good ole' US of A. Their gothic brand of nihilism revved up with a constant flow of devil-worshiping, anti-religious, anti-Ronnie Raygun rhetoric designed to incite maximum outrage had become increasingly effective once they entered the South. Although they'd played more traditional major city dates than the Pistols' ill-fated tour in '78, their manager was clearly enough of a Malcolm McLaren wannabe to have ensured their agent book some small towns they'd been lucky to get out of alive. He, of course, was doing this all from the relative safety of his Soho office in London.

The bus eased down Sixth Street and sidled up to the Driskill Hotel, which had first opened back in 1886 but even in its slightly tatty, faded glory was a huge upgrade from everywhere they had stayed since New York—due, Drea gathered, entirely to the fact that the record company's head of publicity, Suzanne Black, had set up a press day here and was accordingly springing for the rooms.

The bedraggled band and crew shuffled up the steps to the ornate, high-ceilinged, pillared entryway. George, the curly-haired, rotund Glaswegian tour manager, put his arm around Guy's shoulder while they checked in.

"Guy, me and the lads heard it was you who made sure the crew got to stay here too instead of being shipped off to some shite dump as per usual. Top man."

"I tried to get you all danger money for the Southern part of the tour, but these two nights were all I could muster, unfortunately," said the singer.

Drea overheard the exchange and grinned. She really liked these guys, who had known each other for years after attending the same school. For all the outrageous posturing, there was something very genuine about the band as a gang of true friends, which was just what she needed after the horrific experience with the sheriffs and the lingering horrors of the place she'd been kidnapped and locked up in back in Orange County.

She'd called her dad from Chicago and elicited a solemn promise that there would be no further attempts at drastic rehab if she agreed to return to LA. Her instincts had been right and it had been her mother's agent's idea—who was, no doubt, only concerned that he not miss any of his ten percent from the highly paid TV series her mother appeared on every week, if she quit over concerns about her daughter OD'ing.

Drea was just praying the sheriffs would forget about her and James as time passed.

Surely there were plenty of new murders in LA to busy themselves with?

She and Duncan got a couple of luxurious hours to themselves in the beautiful high-ceilinged, sparse, but perfectly appointed room, almost falling asleep together in the giant bath before the phone rang, ending their reverie. Suzanne Black had arrived from New York and wanted to brief the band over lunch.

The band and Drea piled in a giant, late-1950s green Cadillac with Suzanne behind the wheel, the ace publicist clearly knowing all English boys loved old be-finned American cars.

"I'm taking you to see the classic Austin joint, the Armadillo World Headquarters, which you'll be playing at. It's recognized as the first club to draw cowboys, redneck truck drivers, and dope-smoking hippies into the same venue and as a focal point of what became known as the Austin Sound, which merged country and rock. Everyone from Ray Charles to the Clash played this spot but I hear it's closing at the end of the year, so we are just in time."

The wide streets and single-story buildings baking in the shimmering heat were incredibly relaxing to Drea despite Suzanne driving like she was still in New York.

Drea was in the back with Duncan, soft-spoken bass player David, and mostly silent but volatile drummer Ben while Guy rode shotgun, talking animatedly with the New Yorker.

They easily got a table in the sprawling place. A beautiful teenage waitress distributed big menus to them, all of the band clearly transfixed by her classic friendly Southern accent.

Drea and Suzanne exchanged an amused eye roll with each other. Suzanne was clearly a whole different breed than the assortment of big-talking, bullshit-artist, local promotion people who had taken them to radio stations and record stores in other cities. She was dressed in Chanel-inspired business clothes but there was some subtle arty edge Drea felt drawn to.

The orders went in fast: fried catfish (times two), chicken fried pork chop (times two), glazed ham, Southern fried oysters. Then Suzanne laid out the plan.

There was clearly a coconspirator, almost sexual tension between Guy and Suzanne, but Drea would bet the publicist never let that go all the way.

"So, I know my office got you a schedule of the individual interviews we had set up but you've done such a good job pissing off a disparate variety of Southerners that I think we can pull off an old-fashioned press conference. There's just about enough radio airplay on 'Obliteration' to maybe get some local network TV crews out, too. Guy, I have a surprise for you. There are two boxes of Aleister Crowley's *Diary of a Drug Fiend* at the hotel. I thought you would enjoy giving copies to the media and maybe to some kids at the upcoming shows?"

The usually straight-faced singer now wore a devilish smile. "You are truly inspired, Suzanne."

Everyone dove into the almost exclusively fried food with happy abandon. Ben and David's discovery of catfish was clearly life changing. This was washed down with several beers by all but Suzanne, who had bravely ordered white wine. By the time they rolled back to the Driskill, there was barely an hour to spare to get changed for the press conference.

Drea had gotten in the habit of applying Duncan's eyeliner, which gave him a slight edge over the rest of the band. But nonetheless, their head-to-toe all-black attire created just the desired effect as they strode into the banquet room led by Suzanne.

The floor had stunningly classic tiling in soft green and amber. The low, bronze-engraved, ornate ceiling looked deco to Drea, who had grabbed a chair among the press seats. The center of the L-shaped room had a beautiful circular band above, which rose several feet, made of hand-cut glass that had been painted partly in light green and very faded yellow. The black stars that were repeated around the circle gave things exactly the right inference of dark magic.

The band sat at chairs that had been placed directly underneath the circle, creating a vibe that read part inquisition chamber, part pentagram. The media, who numbered around thirty, was a motley mix that ranged from long-haired rock writers to Brooks Brotherssuited TV representing the local affiliates for all three networks. Suzanne masterfully picked the inquisitors from the raised hands to build from affable to inflamed.

"Hi, Dave DiMartino, *Creem Magazine*. Duncan—the Psychedelic Furs and Vortex appear to have formed at almost the same time. Were you perhaps inspired by the same things?"

"Thanks, Dave. We love the Furs but I can't speak for them, although I do wish I'd written the 'America Ha Ha Ha' line. We are responding to the appalling social and political climate we live in that desperately needs extreme change."

"Ben Lee, *Austin Chronicle*. Is that what 'Obliteration' is about?"

"We don't believe in explaining our lyrics. They are whatever you feel from listening, be it obliteration of a relationship or a government. Take your pick."

"Roy Trakin, *New York Rocker*. Guy, you have been very outspoken about both Margaret Thatcher and the Republican presidential candidate Ronald Reagan. Is this just for post-punk shock value?"

Guy, lolling in his chair at his languid, dissolute best, drawled calmly, "We are reflecting everyone's shock, not creating it, Roy. We have a prime minister who has sold a generation down the river and you lot appear to be on the verge of electing a cheesy actor who can't even decide what political party he's in but is sure he wants to drag you back to the morals and repression of the 1950s with some Cold War politics thrown in to keep your attention away from the shit show. We are here to warn the US what it could get like."

Drea had noticed people flipping through the pages of the books that had been left on their seats and now the lantern-jawed, straight-arrow guy from CBS waved his copy in the air and finally attracted Suzanne's attention.

"Yes, Ron, your question, please?"

"Sir, we are led to believe that you have been giving out the deranged writings of a devil-worshiping drug addict to our young folk at your concerts. I, for one, find this despicable. Would you care to explain yourself?"

"Aleister Crowley was a fascinating fellow, as is this book. Overall, I'd say it's a cautionary tale. I believe if it was taught in schools, there'd be far less serious drug addicts, actually," said Guy amiably.

Things devolved into a shamble as Ron sputtered outraged follow-up questions and the rest of the mainstream press took the bait hook, line, and sinker.

Suzanne conducted the circus masterfully, Drea thought, finally leading them all back to the safety of their rooms. She didn't go to sound check but ordered room service with Suzanne and watched the local news. They cracked up, debating how real the TV journalists' outrage was but the on-camera captions were classic: *Junkie rock stars want to preach devil worshiping to our children in schools. The British Invasion we didn't want. Debauched Satanist junkies tell us to vote against American values.*

There was a knock at the door. To Drea's surprise, it was George, Guy, and Duncan. "What are you guys doing here?"

"It's a mite tense outside the gig. Protesters and the like. The boys wanted to make sure you don't have any aggro getting in," said the tour manager.

"So you thought it would be safer if we went in with the object of their anger?" drawled Suzanne.

"We are going to take you in through an entrance in the back. All the action's out front," explained Duncan.

By the time the cab arrived at the Armadillo, there was a good number of angry citizens mixed with the kids lined up waiting for the doors to open.

Drea noticed a couple of quickly made, scrawled banners being held up as they slowly drove by.

GO TO HELL, SATANISTS. DON'T MESS WITH TEXAS, JUNKIE PERVERTS.

It was happily deserted around the back, the small entrance only illuminated by a dim single-bulb light and even that was partly obscured by a large trash dumpster. George paid the long-haired driver and they clambered out, George and Guy close to each other, leading the way. A large crew-cut man came out of the shadows. Drea presumed he was security.

He stepped toward them, pushing back his knee-length black coat to reveal both a huge beer gut and a belt with a holster containing an enormous, old-fashioned Colt 45. He pulled it out, cocked the hammer gunfighter style, and aimed it at Guy's head. "You forgot to tell us how you feel about gun control, you limey piece of shit."

George, who was still next to the singer, took one quick step forward and brutally headbutted the gunman, shattering his nose. The gun and man fell to the ground.

"He also forgot to ask how you feel about the Glasgow kiss, you redneck cunt."

Blood gushed from the man's ruined nose and face as he cursed and whined incoherently.

George kicked him around the ribs and head several times for good measure until he passed out while the rest of them stood frozen in horror at the near fatal moment. George picked up the weapon, holding it by the barrel. "Would you like a wee souvenir of Texas, Guy?"

CHAPTER 11

JAMES'S RECENTLY MET FRIEND from Belfast, Norman, came to pick him up Saturday night. James lugged his yellow milk crate full of records and put them on the front floor of the red VW Bug where the passenger seat used to be. He didn't ask how that state of affairs came to be but given the Irish soul man's general wild, reckless, brawling behavior, he imagined there might be a good story behind it. They headed down Crescent Heights and hung a left on Melrose, going east until Paramount Studios loomed on the left.

The venerable Nickodell restaurant was built into the outside of the studio, which had actually been RKO initially. The place was unsurprisingly busy given its largely elderly clientele's preference for early dining. They entered the dark interior. The aged, formally dressed maître d' led them to a red booth and left two giant menus likely unchanged since the 1950s, as was the rest of this beautiful spot, which always made James feel like he was on an old ocean liner.

They both ordered satisfyingly large Scotches and perused the pale-blue and yellow menu that featured a stunning artist's rendition of the building on the cover.

Joe, the waiter—who, like every other person working in the restaurant, looked as if he had been there since the place was built—arrived. "What is your pleasure, gentlemen?"

"Don't get me started on what my pleasure is, Joe. Just tell me what's good to eat," said Norman.

"I think for you, the steamed Finnan haddie with boiled potatoes. Would you like that à la carte?"

"Bring me the whole fucking cart, with everything on it and the horse that pulled it, Joe."

James went for sand dabs and they agreed on a Caesar salad to start.

Joe quickly returned with a trolley covered in a white linen tablecloth. He made the Caesar from scratch, cracking eggs and using anchovy fillets, mixing everything in a large stainless-steel bowl. James loved this ritual.

"So who's playing at your club tonight?"

"It's a band called the Boxboys. When I started out, they were the only ska band in Los Angeles. Mostly a good bunch of people, too. I think you'll like them. The keyboard player Scott, bassist Ivan, Greg the drummer, and I have been out on the piss a few times after hours, so I figured it's a good night for you to come down."

"Alright, man. I'm ready to rock and roll." Norman downed his second Scotch.

"So how did you end up here?" asked James.

"I was in the merchant navy and jumped ship in San Francisco in '67. You can fucking imagine what a head spin that scene was to a Belfast boy. Had the time of my life with all those women, LSD, and what have you. Got married a year back, so my girl Patricia and I decided to make the move down here a few months back. Reinvent our lives a bit."

"I get it, mate."

They ate fairly quickly. The food was fine but this place was all about booze and ambience, both of which they soaked up plenty of before heading out into the night.

Norman sped them east on Melrose before wending his way up a couple of side streets to Sunset. He dropped James and his crate off and went looking for parking, which was perpetually a bitch around here. James had agreed to let the band have a late sound check and they'd obviously decided to stick around until set time. Greg stood just inside the doorway, talking to Louise the London girl, whom James had hired as cashier at the drummer's suggestion. She and her boyfriend Kalle had been club regulars since the beginning. Greg and Kalle basically modeled themselves visually and attitudinally after Clash men Mick Jones and Joe Strummer, and they pulled it off well.

Norman had got lucky with parking and joined them, so James made introductions before heading beside Louise to open up for the night. She couldn't remember his name but said some angry neighbor—Curtis something or other—had called, complaining about the noise, especially from the kids leaving, but James didn't have time to dwell on that.

There was an instant stream of kids. He'd noticed a few scooters wedged against the sidewalk that no doubt belonged to some of the long, green-parka-wearing, mod-inspired teen regulars who quickly hit the dance floor as he dropped Bad Manners' "Lip Up Fatty."

They had hired a new bartender, Pilar, who was from the neighborhood, super fast, and affable with everyone. James really liked her and hoped she didn't burn out from the insane pace of beer slinging like her predecessors had.

By nine, the place was packed to the gills. He dropped the brilliant plea to Thatcher "Stand Down Margaret" by The English Beat, hoping they wouldn't need to write " Stand Down Ronald" by this time next year.

He zipped down to the dressing room where the Boxboys were waiting.

"You good to go on? It feels extra revved up in here tonight."

Petite singer Lisa bounced around. Affable guitar player Larry said, "That must be because we are here, right?"

Keyboard player Scott, who always kept things organized, was already heading for the curtain. "More than ready, but Greg's still at the bar."

"That's probably my fault. I introduced him to my friend Norman. I'll give him a nudge on my way back," said James.

The crowd was so dense he didn't see them, so he turned his mike on and talked over Desmond Dekker's "007 Shanty Town."

"Is there a drummer in the house? The Boxboys need one on stage."

This got a few cheers and he then saw Greg, beer in hand, pry himself away from Norman and Kalle.

He put on the Spanish language version of Madness' "One Step Beyond" as a nod to the increasing number of local Latino kids who were coming in and the dance floor went ballistic. The band had edged their way round the perimeter wall and onto the stage.

"Are you ready for some 'Uptown Yankee Ska'?"

Scott's signature keyboards kicked in and they started with their beautifully ska'd up version of the Supremes' "Come See About Me." Lisa had replaced an earlier singer, Betsy, not long before, but her growing confidence was evident, plus the band as a whole was super tight on a level Top Ranking was still far from.

One of the young kids James talked music with sometimes pried himself off the dance floor and walked up to the wall James was leaning against.

"Some of us club regulars have formed a band, and I was hoping you'd think about giving us a gig. We were all inspired by the music here and the Boxboys, to tell you the truth."

"Really, Clyde? Happy you are doing it, mate. Have you played anywhere yet?" James was intrigued. Clyde was a really nice guy who was voraciously soaking up vintage soul and ska in a cool, humble way. Plus, you could have dropped him on stage with the Specials and he would fit right in.

"Um, no, nothing like that. A bunch of us have been rehearsing, though. We did record the last one if you might have time to listen sometime?"

"Alright. Bring it next time you come."

Clyde reached into the inside pocket of his razor-sharp silver tonic mohair suit, pulled out a cassette, and handed it to James.

"The Untouchables, huh? Cool name. I'll definitely listen."

He found Norman back at the bar solo as Kalle had hit the dance floor. "Your place is alright, man. I like it but it feels like an inferno in here."

"Imagine you had a parka on like those kids, squire." James nodded at the dense scrum in the center of the skanking crowd.

It was intense tonight, even by "House of Sweat" standards, and periodically drenched dancers would head out onto the street to grab some air before diving back in.

"James, you'd better come out front!" Louise yelled from behind the bar. She never left the ticket window area, so he didn't question her.

"'Scuse me, squire. Let me see what's up."

Standing inside the door was a tall, imposing, uniformed man clearly from the fire department. "Let's step outside, Mr. Dual."

A fire truck, its lights blazing, was double-parked outside. Probably about fifty kids were on the sidewalk in various stages of joyfully wired inebriation and dehydration. "Captain Hollister, Rampart Fire Department. My men have been complaining about you for months, but to be honest, I thought they must be exaggerating the situation here. Now I can see they were grossly understating the ridiculous state of affairs you are presiding over." He took his helmet off and tucked it under his arm, revealing sandy, precision-cut hair that emphasized his lantern jaw and craggy face.

"I believe you are licensed for one hundred and fifty patrons and my conservative estimate would be that there are around four hundred people in that hellhole right now, not to mention these clearly dangerously dehydrated kids, many of whom appear to be underage. They are also obstructing the sidewalk from regular passersby. Are you getting my point, sir?"

"Yeah, it has been quite busy tonight but everyone's having a good time. There's never any trouble inside and in the extremely unlikely event of a fire, we have those huge double doors that open right onto the street," he said with a shake of his head to the left, indicating the large red wooden double doors they used for band gear load-in.

"I don't think you are quite getting the picture, Dual. I'm shutting you down. You either pull the plug on that band and get the huge wooden bar removed from inside the doors double quick and empty the place, or I'll instruct my men to treat this like a fire scene and use their hatchets to tear the doors to shreds. What's it to be?"

"That's outrageous. There must be something we can work out here."

"Are you attempting to bribe me? You couldn't afford it. You have five minutes." James turned on his heel, furious. The Boxboys had just launched into "American Masquerade." He really liked this song and waited for them to finish before turning his mike on.

"The fucking fire department's outside, and they are shutting us down for the night. Sorry, but everyone has to go home."

One girl yelled from the dance floor. "This is our home. Fuck them." This got some cheers.

He put on the Specials' "You're Wondering Now" and flicked on the house lights. No one left the floor, though.

He walked to the stage, where the band still stood. "Sorry, you lot. Nothing I can do. Greg, would you mind helping me open the doors before those fuckwits tear them down?"

The drummer nodded glumly.

"Thanks, mate. Let me get you lot paid up first. Then I'll be back."

Norman left to retrieve his Bug while James and Scott went back to the tiny office behind the bar, settled up the band's split of the door money, and did a couple of lines. They had just agreed to meet up at notorious after-hours club the Zero Zero later when Greg and Ivan flew in through the door, choking and coughing.

"The fucking cops lobbed tear gas grenades into the crowd outside." said Greg. "I've always said there's three things you can do in Silver Lake. You can go to the O.N. Klub, or the corner liquor store, or get shot. In that order. Guess I can add a fourth." said Ivan.

James jumped up and made for the door but Greg said, "Be careful. That shit will take a minute to disperse."

Although seething, James resisted running out and went to get his crate of records before stepping out on the street.

It was total chaos. Kids were running down Sunset in both directions while those who'd got the worst of it sat on the sidewalk, coughing and rubbing their eyes. One mod boy and girl were being tossed face down across the hood of a black-and-white, proving there was no gender bias to the LAPD's abuse of innocent citizens. The fact that most of them were still sweaty from dancing meant the CS gas ran down their faces and into their eyes, causing extreme pain and discomfort.

Hollister looked smugly down from the safety of a fire engine. "I told you five minutes, Dual. You were too slow. This is on you. Authority's a bitch, huh?" Two more Rampart patrol cars were parked across the street.

Norman pulled up and James climbed in, depositing the milk crate as before.

"Let's get you out of here before you go east London on that fireman. The Zero Zero doesn't open until two. Why don't we run by Blackie's and drink there meantime?"

"Yeah, good idea, squire."

James noticed one of the cop cars had slid out behind them after Norman made an illegal U-turn. "Better take it easy."

"Don't get paranoid on me now," said Norman.

The cops stayed on their tail west on Sunset but didn't follow when they turned off. The small club was just south of Melrose on La Brea. James was burning mad and looking for any excuse to explode. They strode in without paying and the guy on the door didn't seem ready to discuss the matter. The small, narrow, tunnellike room had a bar on the left, across from which were a few cocktail tables along with a jukebox, which James immediately fed with a handful of quarters. The tiny stage was at the far end of the room. There were maybe twenty people in there, all told.

After a couple more drinks and a few decent songs like Joe Jackson's "Look Sharp," which summed up James's approach to life these days, his spirits lifted. By the time Squeeze's "Cool for Cats" played, they were singing along at the top of their lungs. Unfortunately for all concerned, a band had taken the stage and their tuning up was drowning out Squeeze.

"We are the Rubber City Rebels." They started in.

James, whose back had been to the stage, spun round in horror. "I fucking hate this band. Get off the fucking stage, you poseur wankers."

He continued a drunken but eloquent dissection of the band who embodied everything he hated about punk bandwagon-jumping shit bands. The Cleveland transplants were so angry by the time their set prematurely ended that the entire band headed straight for James.

"I ought to kick your ass," said the singer.

"That's about as original as every one of your shit songs. Fuck off back to Ohio, you unmitigated wanker."

There was a moment of indecision. Despite the four-to-one odds in his favor, the singer didn't like the evil look in James's eye. Then Norman stood up.

Decision made, the band skulked off.

CHAPTER 12

NORMAN WEAVED AND DRUNKENLY bumped a silver Mercedes Coupe a foot or so to create a parking space outside the Zero Zero's 1955 Cahuenga Boulevard location, which lay in a fucked-up, semi-industrial part of Hollywood.

Art musician Wayzata de Camerone, who had come up with the inspired idea that there had to be somewhere to go after all the legal clubs shut down at two, stood outside. He was tall, wore an open-neck black shirt, and sported his usual large-framed glasses.

"Oi, oi, Wayzata. How's it going?"

"Better since we switched to just Friday and Saturday nights, James. The weeknights were dead."

"I get it, mate. I've always done the same so far."

"I want to play you my band's—the Brainiacs—songs. I think we might fit in with the spirit of what you are doing. You have to hear 'Drunk with Funk.' We don't have a draw, though."

"That don't really matter to me. I think crowds are coming now because they trust the bands will fit in with the records in one way or another."

"Glad to hear you are doing well."

"Not tonight, though. The fucking fire department shut us down and the law tear-gassed the kids on the street."

"So you actually have alcohol here?" asked Norman, who clearly wanted to cut the small talk and continue drinking.

"Wayzata, this is my mate Norman."

The singer pulled out a silver case and handed over a plain white card that simply said "Zero Zero Club" with a four-digit number underneath.

"Here's your membership, Norman. It's usually five bucks for guests. There're two fridges inside. Knock yourself out. By the way, I think that's John Belushi's Mercedes you just dinged up, but odds are he won't notice."

The O.N. Klub's constant uninvited guests were rats and the Zero Zero's were cockroaches. They scurried in droves across the floor of the bare, unadorned, black-painted front room.

James led them through the already filling roomful of punks and assorted miscreants to one of two much smaller back rooms. Norman headed toward one of two red spray-painted fridges.

Rough and ready blues singer Top Jimmy stepped away from a small wooden bar, cut in front of Norman, and pulled out a Schlitz malt liquor. He popped the top and handed the can to the Belfast man. "Tip, please."

Norman glowered at him. "I'll give you a fucking tip, man. Don't fuck with me if you want to keep your head on your shoulders."

"Oi, Jimmy. I wouldn't advise pulling that hustle on this man," James interjected, hoping to avoid a messy brawl. The guy had been pulling this move a lot on punters the past few weeks.

There was a tense standoff until Blasters brothers Dave and Phil Alvin (possibly sensing the situation, being no strangers to fights between themselves) stepped in. Dave put his arm around Jimmy by way of greeting and steered him out of harm's way.

"I'll bang some songs on the jukebox," said James. Defunkt's "Defunkt" was first up.

By three, there was little room to move, with every occupant significantly the worse for wear after a long night of clubbing followed by this joint's cheap beer or, worse yet, the supermarket jugged wine. So much booze was spilled from sloppy drunkenness that the cockroaches were mostly swimming or drowning by now.

Norman sang along at the top of his voice to "Local Girls" by Graham Parker and the Rumour, followed by his fellow Belfast boys the Undertones' "Teenage Kicks."

X had shown up, presumably post-gig, with a bunch of friends and fans, and James noticed John Doe looking concernedly at a couple nodding out on a couch.

"What the fuck's the matter with them?" Norman asked.

"Squire, all of a sudden, heroin seems to be everywhere. It's becoming like a dividing line somehow."

"What do you mean?"

"Well, punk busted down some doors and was a wakeup call to get up and do something with your life for me, ya know, and I think for most everyone here. Somehow, though, it feels like the door's closing again. I ain't saying punk's dead but it painted itself into a corner.

"Most people in this scene won't ever fit into regular jobs, so if you haven't made some inroads by now, things are starting to feel bleak. I don't know where all the smack is coming from this year but there's more and more willing takers."

Norman slapped him on the back. "Cheer the fuck up, man. It's probably your speed wearing off. Wanna get out of here? I'm flying anyway and this beer's shite."

Echo and the Bunnymen's "Villiers Terrace" came on.

James grinned. "Yeah, this is pretty good exit music. And I don't have any more quarters for the jukebox, anyway."

As they pushed through the throng, James saw a torn-fishnet-stockinged leg adorned with a very familiar-looking boot disappear into the tiny loft area. A vampiric figure in a long black leather coat was on the construction ladder a couple of steps behind.

James detoured them in that direction. They scrambled up the ladder unsteadily, Norman cursing as he missed a step. As James's head popped through, he could see the rest of Drea, sprawled across the flea-bitten old sofa with two vampiric figures, one on either side of her.

"Honey. I just got back. This is Duncan and Guy from Vortex."

There actually wasn't enough room to stand upright in the tiny, low-ceilinged room. It was primarily used to do drugs, which, judging by the kit that lay in Drea's lap, was her plan.

"Welcome home," said James.

CHAPTER 13

JAMES CAME TO. HE didn't remember anything from last night after the Zero Zero, but could see some greasy-looking wrapping paper on the floor of his bedroom, so guessed a visit to Dani's Oki Dog or the Orange Julius for chili fries may have occurred. He hoped to God, for his stomach's sake, that it hadn't been Pink's hot dog stand. After one morning when he'd seen them scraping back and breaking the crust on the chili that had been clearly out all night, he'd sworn never to return.

The phone was ringing.

"James, it's Loraine. I just had lunch with Tony in his bungalow at the Beverly Hills Hotel. Can you meet me? I need to talk to you."

"I just woke up, girl. Can't it wait?"

"No. You put me in the room with this guy and you need to see me now."

"Give me an hour or so. Do you mind coming here? I've got a brutal hangover. I don't want to go out until dark."

"The sunshine bores the daylights out of you, right? Okay, give me the address." He'd barely showered and dressed when the buzzer rang forty minutes later.

She wore a dogtooth jacket and matching miniskirt, charisma to burn but looking shaken and not a little angry. James walked her up to his sparsely furnished living room and they sat on the stunning dark-blue Italian leather couch he'd bought on Real Records' dime. "Bumpy's Lament" from the *Shaft* soundtrack was playing low through the Bang and Olufsen speakers on the turntable of his stereo, which he'd also expensed to Real before he left.

"James. You are the first person I've trusted in a very long time. What were you thinking?"

"So what happened? Did he come on to you?"

"He answered the door wearing a red silk robe and when we sat, it became very clear he wasn't wearing anything underneath."

"Fuck. I'm sorry. Then what?"

"You know he wants to manage me, right?"

"Well, yeah. I thought I told you that?"

"I mean he wants to manage me only. Five minutes into the conversation, he told me there's no way the band is good enough to play on my album and that I'd need to ditch them. That I'm much more marketable solo anyway."

"That old move, huh? Well, if you are loyal to them and you feel like it's band as gang—which I absolutely respect and endorse—tell him you're not interested if that's part of the deal."

Her head went forward a little, and she rubbed her hands on her temples. "He's like a fucking snake charmer. He got me talking a little and started telling me all the great things he can make happen, and I already felt trapped."

James thought about how Tony had lured him into the setup. "How so?"

"I let it slip my US visa is up soon, and he said he had pull in all kinds of places and could get me a green card if I wanted. But when I was less enthusiastic about the whole picture, he implied that if he wasn't involved, who knew what could go wrong if I tried to renew my visa. I only have a tourist one. You, and, from what I hear, most clubs, pay in cash so having a work visa hasn't really mattered so far."

"Despite all the insane shit that happened along the way for me, I like it here, and I don't see going back to London. What about you?

72

Reason I ask is, however this plays out, it's not going to be easy. So, you'd best be sure it's worth it to you."

"Well, Jamaica is home but it's even harder there. I grew up in Treasure Beach, which is a little fishing village on the south coast, and everyone struggles. I know the music world thinks Jamaica's all about reggae and spliff but marijuana's not legal and my singing was done in church. They'd call all the music you know from there devil's music.

"I ran away from home at sixteen and headed to Kingston to try to make it as a singer. That was a huge shock to my system. Actually, a bigger one than coming here. Dancehall was coming in hard and all that change is making the music scene full of turmoil but creating opportunities, too. I was on a few tracks as a backup singer, on rootsier stuff mostly. As much as I love dancehall, ska's what I want to record, so it makes more sense to be here or London, right?"

"Yeah. Anyway, I imagine you've seen some pretty hair-raising shit around the Kingston music business, so why has Tony got you so worried and how can I help?"

Her head dipped again, and she paused for a while before speaking.

James got up and flipped the *Shaft* soundtrack over and couldn't resist starting it at "A Friend's Place." Whether it was the track or the moment he would never know, but she surprised him by taking his hand before continuing.

"Look, I was furious and scared when I walked out of that suite. I was angry with myself for trusting you and feeling very alone. I wasn't going to tell you the last part because I couldn't risk you telling Tony but I guess I'm going to take a big chance on you.

"He got a call while I was there. Said he was going to take it in the bedroom. He told me to hang up the living room extension once he picked up. When I heard his voice, I started to, but I did hear a man's voice say, 'The product's moving even faster than expected. Get more shipped now before we run out.' Tony was gone maybe ten minutes. Then he suddenly stormed back in a rage, saying he heard clicks on the line and that I'd been listening in.

"He picked me up by my shoulders, shook me like a rag doll, and then held me up close so we were eye to eye. My feet were dangling eighteen inches off the carpet. I whined like a little girl and promised on my life that I hadn't. He said that's exactly what I was doing and he would remember the promise. Then he put me back down on my chair and went back to music business talk like nothing had happened. James, I hated myself for being so weak. I've been on my own a long time and I truly thought I was a tough girl, but he chilled me to the bone. I just sat there, mutely nodding, until he told me to run along."

"He was probably talking about shipping records for one of his artists. There's a lot of shady shit that goes on. Try to forget about it."

"But if it was just records, why would he threaten my life?"

He leaned in and they eased into a tight, lingering hug. Immigrant empathy had deepened his feelings for her and desire was surfacing too.

Her left hand moved up from the small of his back and gently pulled the hair on the back of his head so he was face-to-face with her. She kissed him hard and long.

James felt anger burn both with himself and for Mr. Tony Marshall. *What the fuck had he got them into?* He got a flash of the baseball bat crashing on that desk.

CHAPTER 14

THEY SAT SILENTLY FOR a while. Then she kissed him again, lightly and questioningly. "If you want me, you'll never have a better chance than right here, right now. I'm sure I will come back to my senses by tomorrow."

The door buzzer rang. A frozen moment as they both thought the same thing. "If it is Tony, I'll try to get rid of him quickly. Why don't you go wait in the bedroom." He pointed to the half-closed door across the small hallway.

He walked downstairs nervously, not feeling ready to deal with Tony just yet. He opened the door. It was Drea.

"Honey, want to come to a dinner for Vortex at Cyrano's before their Roxy show? I've got a cab."

"I'm in the middle of something and a friend's here."

"Bring them if you like. So much to catch up on, and I want you to hang out with these guys. You'll like them."

"Alright. Come up for a minute."

Hearing a woman's voice as Drea and James walked up and into the living room, Loraine came out of the bedroom.

"Oh, that kind of a friend. See you found a way to occupy yourself while I was gone," said Drea with a raised eyebrow and a grin.

Loraine looked daggers at her.

"Drea, this is Loraine. She's the singer for Top Ranking, who've been playing the club."

"So, we both found musicians to play with, huh?" said Drea, completely amused and seemingly determined to make Loraine as uncomfortable as possible.

James knew any attempts at explanations would only make things worse. "Okay. Loraine, please come to Cyrano for this band dinner. It's a really fun restaurant, and I think we could both use the distraction, okay?"

She begrudgingly acquiesced and the three of them piled in the Yellow Cab for the short ride to the Strip.

Cyrano opened in 1958 and was the first really good Italian restaurant to happily welcome rock and rollers, and the crowded tables reflected that. It was a classic Strip space but less formal than most upscale joints. The band was already there, situated in an open-ended round booth, along with Suzanne Black, who had obviously flown in for the critical gig.

Introductions were made and a couple of bottles of Barolo delivered.

Drea, under the pretense of boy-girl seating and that the singers should talk, had mischievously seated Guy between James and Loraine, with Suzanne on James's left. Drea had further confused Loraine by draping herself half over Duncan.

After a couple of glasses of red wine, James was engaged with Suzanne in tales of the road and mainstream media manipulation, and was not thinking about Tony. She was dry humored, cool with an unusual but unmistakable nervous, sensual energy he found intriguing.

He was happy to hear Loraine laughing at something Guy had said, figuring this was taking her mind off things too.

He turned to Guy. "I'm curious about how you got inspired for some of what your band is up to."

"From what Drea tells me about your club, I think you'd understand why we wanted to do something musically different from punk."

"Yeah. I think in our own ways, we are both keeping a punk outlook without getting hemmed in. What about all the satanic aspects? I read that you were giving out Aleister Crowley books. That's pretty brave, down South, I should think."

"If I'd known just how reckless, I might have not gone quite so far there," said Guy ruefully, the gun incident still in his nightmares most nights. "Look, James, honestly, the extent of my devil worshiping is loving Dennis Wheatley novels like *To the Devil a Daughter*. But I do like a lot of other things Crowley had to say."

James laughed. "Fuck, I loved those books too when I was a kid. *The Devil Rides Out* and *The Satanist* were brilliant, right? What made you think to incorporate it into a band, though? I mean, I get Black Sabbath trod that turf but you're nothing like them."

Guy paused, as if making up his mind. "Okay. Dunno why I'm telling you this but did you ever hear of a band called Black Widow?"

"Yeah, I saw them. 'Come to the Sabbat,' right? They did occult meets Hammer horror with virgin sacrifices on stage. You mean…"

"Yeah, it's kind of stuck with me. Don't tell anyone. The *NME* would crucify us."

"Your secret is safe with me, Guy, but I love it."

"What are you boys conspiring about?" asked Suzanne.

"Best you don't know," said Guy.

A dizzying array of dishes arrived in a two-waiter flourish, as plates of veal scaloppini, veal marsala, veal saltimbocca, whole branzino, cannelloni, and fried whitebait were delivered to the semi-drunk gang. An hour or so later, Suzanne dropped her AmEx card on the hefty check and they piled into a stretch limo that zipped them the few blocks west to the Roxy.

There was a healthy line running along the front of the club and by set time, the place was full. James, Drea, Suzanne, and Loraine sat at a table on the raised left-hand section that was reserved by the label for execs and industry people they would be trying to hype the band to. There was a seriously good press turnout, that was for sure.

The band didn't let the pressure of Los Angeles get to them, pulling off their delicate balancing act, both decadent and political in a way James really liked.

The foursome headed up to the private area called On the Rox to join the band for the between-sets forced glad-handing with an array of radio, retail, and press guests.

Guy and Duncan, buoyant from the buzz of a good set, not to mention the wine, amiably played the game. Eventually Suzanne brought them over to the small bar where James, Drea, and Loraine leaned, drinking Harvey Wallbangers.

"Nice job." James grinned.

"What—the show or this tap dance?" asked Guy.

"Both, actually."

Suzanne ordered the same cocktails for herself and the guys, teasing James slightly. "Very LA drink for a London boy."

"Are you here all week? You should come down to my club next weekend. I promise we don't have chichi cocktails."

"Sadly not. I'm flying back in the morning. Coming to New York anytime soon? I'd take you around."

"Maybe. I've been talking to Sylvia Robinson about doing a Sugar Hill rap night at the O.N. Klub and I want to go see what they're up to."

She slid a card from her Chanel purse into his hand, pressing it and her middle finger hard into his palm in a subtly suggestive way. "Make sure you let me know ahead of time."

He glanced at Loraine and Drea, who were now immersed in close-proximity conversation with Guy and Duncan. It suddenly felt like things were getting way too complicated.

Maybe picking up on the same thing, Guy said, "Are you all going to stay for the second set? The label bought most of the tickets for the early show but Suzanne says the late show's sold out with fans. We'll make sure it's a mad one."

"It sounds like fun, mate, but I'm going to bail. How long are you here for?"

"The rest of the band go back to London tomorrow but Duncan and I are going to stay and meet with some possible producers for the next album."

"Alright. You two should come down to the club then. You gotta see Loraine's band."

"Definitely. Definitely," said the singer with a lingering look at her.

"Ready to go, Loraine?" said James.

She stepped toward him and steered them toward a moment of privacy. "I'm going to stay, James. It feels better being in a crowd right now. It's keeping my mind off things. I need that tonight. Do you understand?"

"If you're sure."

She slapped the side of his face gently and gave him a wistful smile. "I told you I'd come back to my senses if you weren't quick."

CHAPTER 15

TWO WEEKS LATER, JAMES sat waiting for Loraine among the hubbub at Cafe Figaro, which was situated at the very west end of Melrose Avenue. He fortunately didn't have a hangover as this joint had the biggest, loudest espresso machine ever. The post-beatnik vibe, newspapered walls, abundant Tiffany lamps, chess sets on tables, and menus printed like broadsheet newspapers with Greenpeace stories on the flip side of the French bistro fare was wacky LA surreal at its most amiable. Two hip hustlers at the table next to him were discussing how they were going to get Hunter S. Thompson's *Fear and Loathing in Las Vegas* made into a movie.

Loraine walked in fifteen minutes late, looking a little bleary, weary, and somewhat worse for wear.

"Jesus, girl. You've aged since the Roxy show."

She feigned a much harder slap than the one she'd left him with when they last saw each other and sat down at the circular wooden table. "You English boys can wear a girl out with your liquor, drugs, and late nights, you know?"

"Yeah? Drea told me you, her, Guy, and Duncan have been out every night except for a few when even she just left the three of you to it. I'm impressed with your stamina."

"James, listen, are you okay? This thing with Guy and me just happened very naturally. He's a truly good person, and it's what

80

I needed right now. He and Duncan have even been taking me to their producer appointments so I'm meeting some amazing people and learning a lot. We are also thinking about doing a male/female cover of Althea and Donna's brilliant 'Uptown Top Ranking.' Please don't be bitter."

"Look, whatever I may or may not be feeling, we don't have time to get into it. I feel responsible for your situation, and Tony's going to be here in forty-five minutes so you'd better let me have a look at this contract he's given you to sign and we'd better have some idea of what you're going to say, alright?"

She pulled a large brown envelope out of her diminutive purse and unfolded it for him.

They ordered double espressos and told the waiter they'd order food when their guest arrived. James plowed through the twenty-page document, nervously keeping an eye on the ornate old clock on the wall across from where they sat.

He looked up with only a few minutes to spare.

"Look, I'm more used to going through label recording contracts than management ones but here's what I can see. There's loads of long-winded shit like all these contracts are laden with but he's asking for twenty percent management commissions on everything, which is okay. What's not typical is that this also has language way deep in there that also signs you to his publishing company, which would own fifty percent of every song you write in perpetuity. In other words, forever. Also, his company has an office in New York but is registered in the Cayman Islands."

"What does that mean?" she asked.

"Ever hear that Members song 'Offshore Banking Business'?" Before she had a chance to answer, Tony was towering over them.

He clapped James on the back while barely managing to slide his long legs under the wooden table. "Good news for you, James. I talked to Big Youth about your joint and if you can work out a deal he can live with, you'll get a show in the fall."

James grinned broadly but also knew he was getting manipulated again. Tony was making sure he was on his side before the main business was addressed.

A black-polo-shirted waiter who seemed maybe a little stoned arrived at their table.

Tony took a quick glance at the oversized menu. "I'll have the cassoulet ragout. What about you two?"

"I'll have the croute au fromage," said James.

"Just more espresso." Loraine looked extremely tense.

"Baby, you need to eat," said Tony patronizingly.

"I'm not hungry."

The waiter hovered uncertainly. "That'll do it," said James.

He caught Tony's expression darken to anger for a split second and then the cheerful mask was back in place.

"I'm back to New York in the morning for Bob's next shows. If we move quickly, Loraine, I can slide you onto a few of the shows by the end of the tour. Have you told your band yet? I'm going to line up some great Jamaican session guys for you in New York. You will love singing with proper players."

"No, I haven't."

"Not to worry. It doesn't really matter. It's not like there's any paper signed between you. Speaking of which, I hope this is signed." He eyed the contract.

She swallowed hard, obviously scared but steeling herself. "No, it's not. I don't feel I can. I know you could speed up my career but it doesn't feel right."

Exaggerated shock bloomed on Tony's face. "James, set this little girl straight. Tell her it's the chance of a lifetime. The one chance in her lifetime, in fact."

The waiter arrived with their order and started to put Tony's plate in front of him. "Go away, boy, and take the food with you. We are busy."

Stoned or not, it only took the guy one look into Tony's eyes to scram.

"Far as I know, managers don't usually take half of people's publishing," said James.

"All Bob's early songs are with my publishing company. He was smart enough to know without me they'd be worth nothing. Do you think you're better than him, Loraine?"

"No. But—"

"Listen carefully. Without me, your songs will be worth nothing. You and your career will be worth nothing. Your time in America will mean nothing, and it also won't last very much longer. With me, you will make a killer record. You will be on shows with the biggest reggae artist in history and you will ride this ska revival all the way to the top and beyond."

He rose. "James, this is your last chance to talk sense into her or our business will also be concluded. Make sure that contract is delivered to the Beverly Hills Hotel before I check out in the morning."

He turned on his heel and was gone.

"Well, that went well, I thought," said James.

Her head dropped into her hands. "What am I going to do?" she groaned.

"You already did it, girl. You stood up to him. I'm impressed. And you did it with a wicked hangover."

"I'm scared, James. He's capable of anything."

"Yeah, I know, but look at it this way. It's not like you owe him money, nor has he invested any real time in you. He'll probably just go back to New York and get on with his business. Think I said bye-bye to Big Youth and Bunny Wailer, though."

She took his hand. "Thanks for being here, James. It means a lot to me. I hope you are right. But what about the call I overheard?"

"I keep thinking about it but haven't come up with anything. Just be careful. Be around people. I'm guessing you aren't at home alone much anyway. Why don't you bring Guy and Duncan down to the club at the weekend? I gave those club regulars in the Untouchables their first show. It should be fun."

CHAPTER 16

HE GOT DOWN TO the club early to find a long row of scooters at the curb outside and a somewhat distressed Louise inside.

"This rat situation is getting worse, James. I throw a barstool into the room when I open up and go into where the light switches are. I can always hear them scurrying away but tonight two of them just sat there, staring me down."

"Fuck. Sorry. I keep telling Bob, and he promises to get something done, but you know how that goes. How was sound check?"

"It was okay. Pretty ragged but they are so excited."

"What's with all the scooters out front?"

"A lot of their friends are already here. They came up from the South Bay and OC."

"Hopefully we'll have a good night. I know the word got around on the street that we'd been closed down."

He hefted his milk crate back to the turntables and started pulling some records.

A few minutes later, Clyde—the band's sharp-dressed, dapper singer, guitarist, and songwriter—came up.

"Thanks for giving us a shot, James. It means a lot, and we won't let you down."

"I know you won't. What song would you like me to play to give you a heads-up it's time to go on stage?"

"Well, we were thinking maybe Secret Affair's 'My World' or something by the Jam."

"Fuck, Clyde. You get what I'm up to here maybe better than anyone else, and you know I'm not into that slavish mod revival retro thing with new bands. Like the Specials and all the 2 Tone acts are moving music forward. I'm not impressed with Secret Affair, and I told Paul Weller what I thought of him back in London at the Roxy one night."

"I understand, James. It's just that a lot of our friends are into them and it would rev things up as we go on."

"Fuck me. I wouldn't do this for anyone else. Tell you what. I'll play "Down in the Tube Station at Midnight," which I have to admit is a decent song."

"Brilliant, James. Thanks a lot."

A rush of parka-wearing male and female kids poured in as soon as the doors opened for business and the club was more than half full within twenty minutes. Way earlier than most of the regulars would usually arrive. James dispensed with the usual slow build of dub and lovers rock and hit them with a lot of early ska: "John Jones" by Rudy Mills, "Fire Corner" by King Stitt, "Wreck A Buddy" by Soul Sisters, "Reggae in Your Reggae" by Dandy Livingstone.

A loud cockney voice yelled from the bar area: "Oi, oi, James! Are you DJing or just playing *Tighten Up Volume 2?*"

James, busted, stepped out from behind the turntables and leaned across the bar where three more recent Freddie Laker arrivals stood, beers in hand.

"Well, Dobbin, you are old, aren't you? This reminding you of your '69 Doc Martins or what?" James said to the shaved-headed, barrel-chested obvious hooligan.

His two builder mates Peter and Lyle were also seriously hard drinkers and sometime bar fighters, but from Liverpool and Newcastle respectively.

"What's with all these cunts in parkas?" Peter looked out at the almost two hundred of them jammed onto the dance floor.

"Easy, Peter. A lot of them just rode up from OC."

"Fucking wankers. We are in California, right? Last time I checked, it was eighty-six degrees today," said Dobbin.

"They are a good bunch of kids, Dobbin. Listen. You know I don't care if you get pissed until you fall down in here, but no aggro with them, okay? They'd be no match and I won't have trouble, alright?"

"Who, us?" Peter asked in his most faux innocent Scouse voice, which was already slurring a little.

"Oh, sorry, Peter, I forgot. It wasn't Dobbin who I stopped headbutting that 2 Tone guy last month."

"James! Look at the turntable!" yelled Louise from the ticket window.

"Excuse me, gentleman. Back to work for me." He turned and looked to where she was pointing. A giant rat was spinning around on top of the classic Trojan album.

As he wondered how to mix in a record on the other turntable and not get bitten, he watched Tom Waits and Rickie Lee Jones walk up and pay Louise. Rickie Lee pulled back the curtain to enter, but seeing the seething mass of dancers turned back and mimed slashing her throat. A heated argument between the singers ensued, causing a bottleneck with the people waiting in line.

Meantime, James managed to seamlessly slide Archie Bell and the Drells' *Tighten Up* onto the other turntable. The rat took its cue and ran up the wooden pole into the dark recesses of the ceiling. James was amused to see Rickie Lee exit and Tom enter.

He cued up "Down in the Tube Station at Midnight" and hit the strobe light. This was the only lighting effect the club had, which was just fine by him. He had a serious soft spot for the strobe and would overuse it for a segment of songs most nights. He'd never used it to usher a band on stage before but figured because they were all regulars used to being bathed in the strobe that they would get a kick out of it.

He could see the band ease their way onto the stage and start plugging in. He grabbed the mike.

"Alright, you lot. For the first time, a band of your own formed from within the Klub. Let's hear it for the Untouchables."

A nice roar went up as they kicked into "Free Yourself." They flew around the stage, very Specials-influenced, but it felt right.

He grabbed a beer and stood on the punters' side of the bar, where he spotted Patrick Goldstein. It was way too loud for a proper conversation but he leaned in, having to almost talk into the journalist's ear to make himself heard.

"Do you know Tony's background beyond managing Marley?" Patrick smiled wryly.

"A little. Did your meeting not go well?"

A uniformed LAPD cop came through the curtain. He scanned the room and used his drawn gun to usher James toward him.

"What the fuck?" said James to Patrick but walked slowly toward the uniform. Forcing a smile, he said, "Sorry. I know it's a bit loud tonight."

"I'm not hear about the noise, asshole. Hands up. Outside now."

James raised his hands over his head and walked slowly to the door. Three other uniformed cops were waiting, guns also drawn.

"Cup your hands," one yelled at him.

"I don't know what that means," said James, way nervous, sensing they were seriously trigger-happy.

A tense pause ensued. Maybe the various sweaty kids catching their breath on the sidewalk saved the easy bullet solution but eventually one cop mimed hands on the back of head and James complied. The one Black cop holstered his gun and patted James down.

"Who the fuck in this neighborhood doesn't know what 'cup your hands' means?" he muttered.

"Sorry. I'm English. Listen, what's this about? I know my club's not popular with you lot, but c'mon."

"We got a call from a homeowner who lives on the hillside above here who said an armed man matching your description broke into his home. He and his boyfriend said they saw you run down the hill and into the club."

"That's crazy. First off, I've been here for hours."

"Shut up, son." He looked up. "He's clean."

The cops seemed to calm down slightly. The search cop cuffed him, though. "We are going to take you in, kid, and get to the bottom of this."

James looked up in exasperation and noticed something. "Wait a minute. Look up at the angle of the entrance here. There's no fucking way anyone living on the hillside up there could see it or anyone entering down here."

The cops all looked up.

"Hate to say it, but he's right," said the cop who'd come into the club.

Louise came out the front door, having obviously decided that under the circumstances leaving the door unattended was okay. "Why is he handcuffed?"

"What's it to you?" asked the cop who had come into the club.

"It's his club, and I work the door."

"When did he arrive?" asked the search cop.

"About seven thirty p.m."

"Are you sure he never left?"

"Of course. He would have had to walk right past me."

The cop pulled James's wallet from inside his long tonic, mohair gray jacket and checked his ID. "Okay, Mr. Dual, we are going to cut you loose for now while we further investigate with the property owner. We may need you later."

The search cop uncuffed him.

James, relieved but moving on to indignant, said, "How does filing a false report go down with you? Who is this guy, anyway?"

"Take it easy. He's a respected real estate agent who is trying to improve the neighborhood, unlike some people."

Louise took James's arm. "Let it go, James." The cops got into the patrol cars and split.

"What the fuck was that really all about?" he wondered out loud.

He and Louise stood alone for a moment as the kids had all gradually snuck back inside while the cops had been there. Given the odds that they were all holding speed of some kind and likely underage, it was probably wise.

A Yellow Cab pulled curbside just up the block, as the line of scooters directly outside were blocking everywhere else, and out piled Drea, Duncan, Guy, and Loraine.

Duncan and Guy were virtually in stage clothes and absolutely at their sartorial best.

Loraine, with her arm round Guy's waist, was dressed in exactly the same outfit from when James had met her. Drea sported a classic black leather jacket.

Guy smiled at James. "You are at the funky end of Sunset Boulevard, I see. Some nice art deco places round here, though, eh?"

A matte-gray '51 Ford Custom 350 Vortec with tinted windows pulled up. Front and back windows rolled down. Gun barrels poked out. Louise screamed. Guy threw Loraine to the ground. Bullets crashed into his vampiric coat, piercing his chest in multiple places.

Blood sprayed over James and Duncan. Drea dove toward the car, cursing. The car peeled out. Loraine crawled to where Guy's body had landed. She put her hands under the stricken singer's head and lifted it slightly. His eyes opened, and he tried to say something to her, but all that came out of his mouth was blood.

CHAPTER 17

LOUISE RAN IN TO call 911. Drea was repeating "motherfuckers" over and over again into the darkness. Blood splattered James, and Duncan, still mute with shock, leaned over Loraine as she whispered to Guy.

"Don't try to talk, baby. Save your strength. Help is on the way. We just need to get you to a doctor."

The sound of the Untouchables was still coming from within when a black-and-white, closely followed by a siren-blaring ambulance, pulled up.

An incredulous search cop and his partner got out, surveying the scene. "What the hell have you been up to now, Dual?"

"It was a fucking drive-by, you idiot!" yelled Drea.

The paramedics eased Guy onto a stretcher. Loraine somehow convinced them to let her go in the ambulance with them.

"We are going to need statements from all of you. Are you the only witnesses you know of?" the cop asked them.

James, remembering Louise's visa had expired and hoping to keep her out of trouble, said, "Yes."

The cops ushered the three of them into the patrol car and took them to the LAPD Rampart Division on West Temple, where they were all put in separate interview rooms.

Thirty minutes later, Detective Sergeant Franc Mata strode into the dingy room that stank disturbingly of disinfectant used to mask

God knew what. "Figured I'd see you in here sooner rather than later, Dual. But murder, huh?"

"What the fuck are you talking about?" said James.

"Your boy was DOA. I haven't got it all put together yet but earlier tonight you were busting into a real estate guy's place above your shithole of a club, waving a gun around. You must have somehow stashed it by the time our boys searched you but ten minutes later, a man's dead and by the looks of it, you're covered in his blood. You look perfect for this jacket to me."

"That sounds about right, Franc. I must have stashed the gun again, right? I'm a part-time magician, so it would be easy. Where do you think it might be and what do you think my motive was?"

"Once we identify the dead guy who wasn't carrying ID and talk to your friends, I'll get back to you on that."

"I'll do you a favor, Franc. His name's Guy Harding, and he's the singer for an English band called Vortex. He was on his way to the club when he was shot in a drive-by from a gray fifties Ford Custom that pulled up outside the club."

"Did you know him?"

"I met him briefly a couple of times out and about the last few weeks. Is he really dead?"

"Yeah, he's dead. You sound remorseful. Guilt eating you alive already?"

"You know this is bullshit, Detective Sergeant, so if you don't mind, I'd like to get myself and his friends out of here. You don't need to drive us but maybe you can call a cab. If I can help you once you start investigating real suspects, I will. He was a good guy, and I'm guessing this was random. He hadn't been here long enough to make enemies."

The cop turned on his heel without further comment and left James cooling his heels, wishing he could wash the blood off.

Maybe an hour later, the door opened again.

"Okay, your story matched the others'. I'm going to kick you loose for now but I will be in touch soon."

"Aren't you going to tell me not to leave town?"

"For that, you can go find your own cab out of here at this time of night. I hope someone takes you out and saves me the trouble."

James was ushered out to the booking area where Drea, Loraine, and Duncan sat, waiting mutely on a wooden bench. James called Yellow Cab and asked if they could get Lenny here ASAP.

Insomniac Lenny came through, despite it being 4:00 a.m. Once they were safely sardined into the cab heading west on the 10 Freeway toward La Cienega, James said quietly to Drea, "I'll call Suzanne Black. She'll know the best way to handle the media. As cold as this sounds, we'd better make sure there's no dope in Guy and Duncan's suites. Once the cops start investigating, odds are they'll hear about the band's rep. Are you up to handling the drug search before you sleep?"

She gave him a slightly insulted look. "Who's better qualified than me to find the drugs, right? Consider it handled."

Duncan and Loraine still hadn't spoken, but they had both turned toward James, so he pressed on.

"Duncan, can you handle calling your manager in London? Someone's going to need to break this to Guy's family before news gets out."

"Yes, I'll call him. Not sure I want to be the one to call his parents. They've never been that keen on me or the band."

Drea looked at Loraine. "Honey, do you want to go home? Or you can stay with me and Duncan if you like?"

"I was thinking I'd like to sleep in our bed at the hotel one more time. You know, just feel close to him, smell him on the sheets so I don't forget too quick."

Lenny had them up to Sunset in a flash with nothing on the road and turned off the Strip onto Alta Loma, where half a block south sat the rock-star haven Sunset Marquis hotel.

James asked Lenny to wait.

Way more discreet than its noisy neighbor, the Hyatt ("Riot") House, this joint enabled its guests to enjoy their debauchery in private, especially if you had a small villa away from the main rooms that circled the outdoor pool, which apparently Guy and Duncan had been indulged with. Guy's door had a Do Not Disturb sign on it, which meant that the room was in exactly the bedraggled state he and Loraine had left it in. She entered, leaving James, Duncan, and Drea to hover in the doorway. Loraine walked through the living room, idly touching a green velvet jacket that was draped over the arm of the couch. She continued through into the large modern bedroom. The top sheet and feather comforter were in separate rumpled bundles. Empty wine bottles were on both bedside tables.

She walked around the perimeter, disappearing into the bath-room for a minute before reappearing and stopping at the side of the bed. She knelt on the floor, burying her head in the luxuriant pillow, and James could hear a muffled sob. With her hands on the bed, she forced her face deeper into the pillow, almost as if she were trying to smother herself.

James motioned to Drea, and they took a step away from the doorway. "I think you should go through the room and make sure there's no dope of any kind here. Once you've checked, call housekeeping and have them service the room. Do the same with Duncan's room. They'll be working in an hour or so anyway. It's hard to say how the law will deal with an investigation, but none of us need that aggro on top of everything else, right?"

She nodded.

"Sure you're okay to deal with all this?"

"Yes. But I think you should get Loraine out of here."

He glanced back in and saw Loraine in the same position. He knelt next to her. He couldn't hear her breathing. He put a hand on her shoulder. "Loraine. Can we talk?"

She didn't respond for a minute but then gradually turned her tear-stained face toward him.

"I'm worried that the police might end up here before long. Would you like to come to my place? I'll crash on my couch."

With her teeth pressed on her bottom lip, she nodded. She got up and walked around one more time, almost the way one might to make sure you hadn't forgotten anything before checking out. He figured she was making sure she remembered the life with the singer she had now lost.

CHAPTER 18

JAMES HANDED LENNY A wad of bills by way of thanks for the taxi driver's nocturnal help as he and Loraine stepped out onto Fountain and the welcome sight of his apartment.

He felt desperate to wash Guy's blood off himself but asked her whether she wanted to shower first. She spoke for the first time since the hotel.

"Yes, please. Do you have some pajamas I can wear too?"

"Sorry. I haven't worn pajamas since I was eleven. Would a T-shirt work?" She smiled wanly and nodded.

He led her through the bedroom to the stunningly preserved deco red-and-white tiled bathroom and started the temperamental taps to make things easy.

He got her the longest T-shirt he could find and went back to the living room.

He pulled the business card Suzanne Black had given him out of his wallet. Her home number was scrawled on the back. By now it was about eight thirty Sunday morning in New York. Although he hated to call or be called at such an ungodly hour, needs must.

She answered on the fourth ring, her voice sounding husky with sleep. "Suzanne, it's James Dual. Really sorry to call so early but..."

"James, are you in town? Want to have breakfast now that you've woken me up?" she said teasingly.

"I wish, Suzanne, but listen. There's no easy way to say this but Guy was shot and killed a few hours ago outside of my club."

"Oh, God, no. Was it a religious nut? I've been scared something like this might happen ever since Texas."

"He was shot from a passing car, so we have no idea," said James, who, until now, hadn't thought about that possibility. "I know this is a horrible shock, Suzanne. You are pretty much the first person to know, and I figured you would know how to handle things. I think Duncan will call their manager but it could be difficult for him here once the press finds out. And, of course, George and the crew went home after the Roxy gig, so there's no one to protect him."

She cleared her throat and sniffed. James couldn't tell whether she was crying or still waking up, but after a moment, she spoke decisively.

"Okay. First thing—we need to make sure any drugs are cleaned up in case the police decide to explore."

"Yeah, I thought of that. Drea's handling it."

"Okay, if you think she really will. I'll call management, too, and deal with the label here. Do you have a contact with LAPD? We are going to need to get a press release out and it's probably best to keep on their good side if possible."

"Yeah, good idea. It's way too late for me as they've been all over the club like a cheap coat but I'll give you Detective Sergeant Mata's number. He didn't know who Vortex was so he didn't immediately go to any dark places but I'm sure he'll get there."

"I think it's okay to leave Duncan at the Marquis for now. They won't let press people in but if it gets bad with TV crews and fans, I'll get him moved to somewhere more secluded, like the Hotel Bel-Air."

"Thanks, Suzanne. I'll let you know anything I hear, but for now I'm going to try to crash for a bit."

Loraine walked out, wearing his terrace bootleg Manchester United shirt commemorating their 1977 FA Cup Final win over Liverpool. "I left the shower running for you."

He walked into the steamed-up bathroom, shed his clothes, and watched the traces of Guy's blood wash away down the drain.

95

He flashed on talking to the singer about Hammer horror films and blood sacrifices, wondering what on earth they'd conjured up.

She was in his bed when he came out with a big towel wrapped around his waist.

"James, it's fine to be in here with me. It'll be light soon, and you'll get woken up on the couch."

He didn't argue but slipped on some underwear from his art deco chest of drawers before climbing in beside her. Surprisingly, he passed out quickly.

He woke disoriented, feeling her pressed against his back with one arm around his waist. He turned to face her. She was awake. She looked scared, her eyes wild and wet with tears.

"I feel like a ghost, as if I died, too, back on the sidewalk," she whispered. He sat up a little, leaning on an elbow, and looked into her eyes. "How can we be sure we are still here and not ripped apart by bullets?" she said.

"Look, girl, Los Angeles reality doesn't operate like anywhere else. It's a surreal dream place. Fact and fiction constantly blend. Maybe you are just starting to realize that."

"James. Fuck me."

"Loraine. It's the wrong reason and time. We can…"

She pulled the T-shirt off and put her hand over his mouth, cutting off his wannabe noble speech about how this could ruin any chance they might have in the future.

"I have to know I'm still alive and this is the only way to be sure." She pushed him on his back.

CHAPTER 19

THE PHONE'S INCESSANT RINGING finally woke him; his blackout curtains ensured there was no way to tell the time. Loraine was sprawled face down, her stunning ass a beautiful reminder not to bother trying to be noble in the future.

James got up and wandered into the living room, which was flooded with late-afternoon sun. The circular art deco clock on the wall read five forty-five.

He rewound the answering machine and found messages from a variety of people who'd been at the club last night as well as Drea, Suzanne, and a naturally worried Louise.

He got some fresh orange juice from the fridge and considered adding some vodka from the bottle of Kamchatka that sat next to it, but decided to wait until Loraine woke up.

First he called Suzanne. She was all fast, highly efficient business.

"Okay, James, here's the latest. It all took a while, being Sunday, but I called your detective sergeant and made nice. They want to go over the crime scene and investigate with as little interference as possible so didn't immediately release anything to the press about Guy's identity. Apparently drive-by shootings aren't that uncommon around there but I guess you know that. Our lawyers are trying to get his body released so that he can be flown home for a funeral. They are also trying to pay whomever they need to avoid an autopsy and the inevitable drug cocktail news being part of the story."

"Really? Labels aren't exactly renowned for that kind of sensitivity."

"You probably didn't know but Guy's parents are part of an extremely well-connected, old, upper-crust family. His father's Lord Harding, and our English label head made it clear it would be best all 'round to spend the money."

"Think it will work since the cause of death is all too obvious?"

"Probably. Money and implied power usually work quite well in cities like ours."

She sounded so ostensibly normal James asked, "Are you doing okay?"

"Honestly, none of this seems real yet, so I'm doing what I can to handle all the label's responsibilities without showing any emotion."

"How come?"

"You have no idea what it's like being a woman in this den of sexist pigs. They'd devour me at the slightest sign of weakness."

"I worked at Real Records until recently, so I get your point."

"He was so sharp and larger than life. It just doesn't seem possible. Who would want to destroy him?"

"There's a lot I don't know right now, Suzanne, but I promise to let you know anything I find out. Hang in, okay? Are you coming out?"

"Thanks, James. I'm not coming now unless Duncan's falling apart. Do you think Drea will be able to keep him on track?"

"Yeah. She's tougher than you might imagine and thinks fast on her feet, no matter what she may have consumed at any given moment. Soon after we met, I fell flat on my face outside the Whisky and two cops were about to take me in. Drea hauled me up. Told them I was English and had been over-celebrating Manchester United beating Liverpool in the FA Cup Final. The match had been months ago, too, so pure invention on her part. Said she was taking me home, whispered run to me, and dragged me stumbling back up the Strip before the bemused cops could react."

"Well, that conjures up quite an image, James. I'll call Duncan and if it gets to the point I need to be there, let me know."

He hung up as Loraine wandered out of the bedroom, rubbing the sleep out of her eyes.

She came and leaned into him. He put his arms around her and felt the still-blazing afternoon sun focus him. *Time to start fighting back. Where to begin?* Last night's insanity swirled like a waking noir nightmare. Everything felt so random except that real estate neighbor who'd filed the fake report. That was tangible. He hated to invite more contact with Franc Mata but maybe it was time to see whether he was a by-the-book honest cop or something else altogether.

He led Loraine to the kitchen, where they put toast on and he used his old tin stovetop espresso maker to wake them up a bit, still forgoing the tempting vodka.

They buttered and jammed the toast and sat on barstools at a small, circular white table.

"You up for talking a bit?" he said. She nodded.

"I just talked to Suzanne, and she's trying to help arrange a London funeral," he said, forgoing any potential autopsy aspect to spare her that grisly visual. "Do you want to be there, Loraine?"

Her teeth pressed on her bottom lip pensively. "I should decide when I can think more clearly. I'm not sure I'd be welcome. I'd like to talk to Duncan about that. In truth, my visa's running out, so since I won't be receiving Mr. Tony Marshall's assistance, I will need to leave the country soon anyway and hope they will renew my visa when I come back."

"Yeah, I'd forgotten about that. I'm well lucky Real Records got my green card sorted. Dealing with that shit can be a real nightmare."

He instantly regretted his choice of "nightmare" but her eyes just raised, and she smiled ruefully at him.

"Don't worry. I know I'm still alive today and these things have to be discussed."

He wiped the toast crumbs off his mouth, threw down the rest of the espresso, and dialed the number on Mata's card. He asked for the detective and identified himself.

After a brief pause: "Dual, I must admit I didn't expect to hear from you."

"Yeah, well, on reflection, I'm trying to give you the benefit of the doubt that perhaps you're just doing your job. Anyway, I'd like to talk to you about last night."

"Really. You ready to confess?"

"Very funny. No, I want to talk about the guy who filed the false report on me."

"Okay. Be here in the morning. I'll cut you some slack and we'll say eleven."

"Can't we talk now?"

"No. It doesn't work that way. Just be here. In our new spirit of cooperation, I'll give you a heads-up, though. We wrapped up at your crime scene of a club an hour ago and released details about the shooting to the news media, so now you're gonna be really infamous."

"Gee, thanks, Franc. You're all heart." The line clicked and went dead.

He called Drea at the Sunset Marquis and filled her in. They agreed that he and Loraine would head over once he'd seen Mata in the morning. He let Suzanne know word was out and went to find the Kamchatka.

He mixed them Harvey Wallbangers.

"Listen, I never watch the local news but I need to see if they pick up on this and if so, how it's being reported. Are you up to it?"

"Yes, James. I have to start putting my armor back on. It all got stripped away last night. You've seen it torn off me twice now, first by Marshall and now by death. No one has ever seen me that naked before, you know? If I don't toughen up again right away, this could all destroy me."

He turned on Channel 7 ABC Eyewitness News as the clock hit 11:00 p.m.

"Christina Hennessey reporting live from Silver Lake." She stood outside the club, where yellow tape cordoned off the area, including the outlined spot where Guy had died.

100

"I'm standing outside the infamous O.N. Klub where a series of ongoing legal brushes with the LAPD and the fire department culminated in the shooting death of British rock star Guy Harding, singer for the devil-worshiping band Vortex, who was gunned down here in the early hours of this morning. In a closely related story, our investigative reporters discovered that earlier James Dual, who is responsible for opening the club, was arrested by the LAPD under suspicion of armed robbery in the home of a respected real estate agent who lives nearby. Unconfirmed reports from ABC sources suggest that Dual, along with guitar player Duncan Edwards, Drea Dresden, daughter of divorced actors Michael and Dolores Dresden, and Loraine Sulley, vocalist for the group Top Ranking, were all present at the scene of the murder."

CHAPTER 20

JAMES AND LORAINE WALKED up to the foreboding Rampart Division entrance just before the appointed hour. They'd agreed she would wait in the lobby while he met with Mata.

James wasn't sure whether it was a good or bad sign that he was walked back almost immediately. He definitely didn't think that being put in a similar interrogation room to the other night was a good sign, though, especially as this one had a glass mirror that he presumed was one-way.

Mata joined him twenty minutes later.

"Wow, Detective Sergeant. I thought our new spirit of friendly cooperation would mean we'd hang out in your palatial office and talk. Maybe even drink."

"Stow it, Dual. I let your lazy rock and roll ass lay in bed and come in at eleven. Besides, my cubicle is buried in paperwork created by losers like you."

"Don't you know people like me sleep until at least noon? Anyway, I imagine in that cubicle is the false report from that real estate guy. I've never met him, so why would he phone in a description of me knowing it could get me killed?"

"Let me get this straight, Dual. You're here because you are pissed off about that, not because you want to help me find who killed Guy Harding?"

"Of course I'm pissed off, but considering his report and Guy's murder happened minutes apart, don't you think there could be a connection? What's this geezer's story anyway?"

"Curtis Manthorne's a real estate agent who has been investing in restoring dilapidated properties in Silver Lake and selling primarily to people in his community—the gay and lesbian community, that is."

"That sounds like you are reading from a press release. How's the LAPD feel about it, really, considering your history? Someone told me that back in the late 1960s you lot went in undercover during New Year's Eve at the Black Cat Tavern gay bar only ten blocks from my club and ended up beating up and arresting a bunch of men. I'm surprised gay people would want to live here."

Mata shrugged. "Old news and before my time on the force. Things change, occasionally for the better. What do you care, anyway?"

"I'm just curious why you seem to have his back. Why haven't you dragged his ass down here? What could he have against me? There's plenty of gay and lesbian couples who like to go to the club."

"Dual, as much as I hate to admit it, you've been given a free pass by the longtime Latino community here mostly because you've welcomed local kids in, and from what I understand, comped them when they didn't have the money to pay. Manthorne, on the other hand, may think a loud club with four hundred kids of every ethnicity spilling onto the street will make the hood look too wild for prospective buyers."

"The LAPD and gay men—strange bedfellows indeed."

The metal door to the interview room crashed open. First through was sheriff's homicide detective Fred Ostrow, quickly followed by his partner Johnny Holton, who, moving fast (considering the heels on his pointed yellow snakeskin cowboy boots), grabbed James by the throat.

"Watch your fucking mouth when you're in police custody, you piece of shit," said Holton.

"Whoa, Johnny—you get lost on Lankershim coming home from seeing Eddie Rabbitt out at the Palomino Club? I like the new country look, though." James barely got the words out as Holton squeezed tighter.

"Get your hands off him, Holton. We can handle our own police brutality, thanks," said Mata.

Holton begrudgingly stopped choking James and took a seat next to the other sheriff's homicide dick Fred Ostrow, who was still dressed fifties-era *Dragnet* style.

"So, Dual, in a rare attempt at cooperation between the LAPD and the sheriff's department, I allowed the detectives here to 'observe' as they have a prior interest in you," continued Mata.

James rubbed his neck. "I bet they have. I have one theory I'm not certain about, though, so let me ask Detective Holton a question first. Do you have such a thing for John Travolta that you switched your *Saturday Night Fever* suit for an *Urban Cowboy* one or are you just a sartorial trendsetter all by yourself?"

"You're going down, you fucking clown. You'll never see the light of day again. We know you were responsible for the Confederacy band's plane crash, and lo and behold the next rock star to die in LA is standing next to you when it happens. We are going to nail you to the wall for this one, and you'll eventually crumble and give us the truth about the crash too. You are going to love prison life so much you'll crawl on your hands and knees to beg us to listen to the truth after a few days," said Holton.

"You are making my fucking dreams come true, Johnny. You got me pegged as a degenerate punk rock kid, rock and roller— whatever the fuck cliché you want to put on me. But I grew up reading Raymond Chandler and Dashiell Hammett, so all your threats and stupid theories when we spend time together are like reading my favorite books or watching films I love come to life. I thought I'd been born too late, but you witless, corrupt cunts are just the same as you ever were, so this all feels perfect to me. You got no murder weapon, no motive, and the only witnesses tell the same story as me. Plus, the FBI don't consider me a suspect in the Confederacy crash."

"Enough, Dual. I'll ask the questions. You have any idea why anyone would want to kill Harding?" said Mata.

"I only met him socially a few times. He was a really nice guy and seemed to get along with everyone around him. They were courting controversy in their press interviews, though. Their publicist, Suzanne Black, told me there was an incident in Austin where some crazed redneck with a gun came after him outside a gig because he didn't like their political point of view." He glanced at Holton. "No offense with the redneck crack, Detective."

A seething daggers look was the only response.

Mata interjected. "Did she say what happened to the assailant?"

James, forgoing the graphic "Glasgow kiss" description, said, "The tour manager disarmed him but I don't think any charge was filed or that anyone found out who he was."

"Ms. Black reached out to me already so I will look further into that possibility via her."

"What about the random drive-by possibility?" asked James.

"It's unlikely. Drive-bys aren't by nature random, and as far as my sources know, the local gangs don't have any issues with you or your club, so the shooting it up for fun doesn't fit. You got anything else?"

"I've given you all I know."

"That'll do it for now. You can go."

Ostrow, who had remained silent until now, said, "We have history with this clown. Give us a crack at him."

"This is my case, Detective, and I extended you a great courtesy allowing you to even be here. You got a beef with him about an old case—handle it on your territory and your own time, not mine. We can discuss anything else after he leaves," said Mata.

"Thank you, Detective." James rose while he had the chance but couldn't resist a parting shot at Holton.

"I will give you one tip, Johnny. Get yourself over to Nudie's Tailors for a proper country shirt and jacket. That Kmart gear's letting your fine new boots down."

He moved quickly to the door and on to the lobby, where he saw a clearly distraught Loraine.

"Sorry. I shouldn't have brought you here." She shook her head and led him out.

Once they were safely back on the street, she turned and faced him, putting her hands just below his shoulders. "Soon after you went in, two plainclothes cops walked in, talking about you. I swear on my life, the one with the yellow snakeskin boots had the same voice I overheard on Tony Marshall's phone that day at the Beverly Hills Hotel."

CHAPTER 21

JAMES HAD ARRANGED TO have breakfast with laconic *LA Times* music columnist Patrick Goldstein at the writer's favorite breakfast joint, the House of Pies on Franklin and Vermont. Hard to miss with the huge house-shaped sign hanging high above its perpetually over-lit interior.

The smog seemed denser, dirtier, and more oppressive in this run-down part of town than in neighborhoods like Beverly Hills, as if even the air quality could be purchased in Los Angeles.

After navigating the wise-cracking trans hookers on the corner, he found the writer already in a booth, drinking coffee.

"How's it going, Patrick?"

"Well, my bungalow down the street's just been broken into for the second time this year and the bastards also stole the front passenger seat out of my VW. But from what I hear, I may still be doing better than you."

"Fuck, I'm sorry, mate, but yeah, I am not doing great either."

A peroxide-blonde waitress of indeterminate age arrived at their booth; her ingenue pretty looks were faded but you could still see the promise of what might have been.

"James, this is Claudette, the woman I'm going to marry one day," said Patrick.

Claudette grinned. "Yeah, once you make editor down at the *Times*, we can discuss that. Meantime, what'll you boys be having today?"

"Apple pie à la mode, Claudette, along with a dinner date Saturday, please."

"That shouldn't be tough, baby, since, as you well know, I work here Saturday nights," said Claudette.

James, who had long wondered what "à la mode" meant, asked for the same. "So, what have you heard about the shooting?" asked James.

"Only what I've read in the paper. The Untouchables were so loud no one heard the shots inside the club."

"I want to fill you in on what happened when that cop took me out. We get outside and there's four of them, guns drawn on me. They say I've just attempted armed robbery on this real estate geezer on the hill above."

"You're kidding me?"

"I know, right? They would have dragged me off except I pointed out this guy couldn't have seen me run into the club as the hillside covers any view of the doorway. So they let me walk and all four cops drove off. But right after, Guy and Duncan from Vortex arrive by cab, with Drea and Loraine from Top Ranking. A minute later, a fifties motor drives up. Two shooters go off and kill Guy, and here we are. There's so many angles to look at this all from, but with the false robbery report and the shooting being just minutes apart, it's hard for me to believe it's purely coincidence."

Patrick shrugged. "There's so much crime here it's hard to say. But let's face it—the way you dress and look is somewhat unique, for LA at least, so the real estate agent must have intended for the cops to come take you away."

"Right? Yeah, I pushed that angle with Detective Mata when I was interviewed about the murder. He wouldn't give me much but sounds like this character's out to do some gentrifying while making himself rich. Mata figures the club might be viewed as an impediment to that."

"Gee, but saying you were armed could easily have got you killed. Seems a bit much if that's all it is."

"Patrick, I know music, not murder, is your beat, but could you ask around at the *Times*? Find out what the story is with this guy and also if your Metro writers have any theories about Guy's murder? Mata wants the club gone badly, so I don't think he's going to do a damn thing about the false report. And the police don't seem to have any idea about the murder except that Mata doesn't think it was a random drive-by as the club itself seems to be in good standing with the local gangs. Guy was almost shot in Austin by some Reagan-supporting, Christian gun lover. I know there's every kind of crazy in Los Angeles but somehow, I don't buy the same thing happening here."

"There's a few Metro possibilities but there's a new, smart, young reporter I met recently, Denise Hamilton, who knows your neighborhood well, so she's probably our best bet."

"Brilliant. Can you arrange for us to meet?"

"Let me talk to her first. If she helps you, she's going to want all you know in return, so you'd best be ready to come clean with her."

"Fair enough. There is one other aspect to this I'd like to pick your brain about and then we can decide."

Claudette arrived with their pies, which looked good, although James was vaguely disappointed to see that à la mode simply meant with ice cream.

"So what's Tony Marshall's story? You know him, right?"

"Real noir character. I figured you'd like that."

"A little too real noir. He stopped on the way to our lunch for a quick spot of threatened grievous bodily harm and demanding money with a baseball bat, which he demonstrated by demolishing a receptionist's desk up on the Strip. After I was stupid enough to set him up to meet Loraine from Top Ranking, he ended up threatening her life if she didn't sign her career over to him."

"You think he's connected to all this somehow?"

"I'm not sure what to think. I actually figured it was unlikely but something else happened that I can't get my head around."

"Let's hear it."

"Mate, I fully trust you but if I tell you this part it can't be shared with anyone—especially your colleagues. I may not know what it's all about but I have zero doubt Marshall's capable of casually killing any of us without a second thought, and I can't further expose Loraine to that."

"Gee, since you put it that way, I'll stifle my fearless reporter instincts for the duration of this conversation."

"Okay. So Loraine's in Marshall's Beverly Hills Hotel suite. Picture him wearing a robe and nothing else to start the intimidation. He gets a call and tells her to hang up once he picks up the bedroom extension. She does but overhears the caller asking Tony to 'up the shipments.' He comes back out, convinced she's listened to the whole call. Shakes her like a rag doll while she pleads and denies, ultimately implying she's dead if she's lying.

"When she tells me, I figure they are discussing album shipments on the Marley record or one of Marshall's other clients but can't see why it's such a dark, secret conversation.

"Flash forward to days after Guy's murder. I'm back in with Detective Mata in a Rampart interview room and Loraine's waiting in the lobby when two hardcore sheriff's department dicks who are still on my case for the Confederacy plane crash enter, discussing me. She's flat-out certain one of them, Johnny Holton, is the voice on the other end of the call with Marshall.

"Now, I just don't see how this asshole could be involved in the record business, even on a crooked level. But if not, what was the call about?" said James.

"On the surface, I don't either. Here's what I do know about Marshall. Even though he's American and born in the South, he's had his fingers in the Jamaican record biz since the sixties. He grew up on the East Coast, primarily New York.

"For years, I've heard rumors his partner in the publishing business is Paul Castellano, head of New York's Gambino crime family, but I've never been able to confirm it. So, take your pick of which illicit side business the charming and talented Tony Marshall could be involved with."

"Great. So we have a mobbed-up record man, vindictive real estate guy, and likely bent cops, all of whom have murderous tendencies and a potential desire to see me dead."

Patrick took a carefully composed bite of equal parts crusty apple pie and vanilla ice cream. "Yep, I think you are about right."

CHAPTER 22

NEWS VANS FROM THE three networks, plus local stations five, nine, eleven, and thirteen, were scattered along Alta Loma as James walked in the blazing sun up the entryway to the Sunset Marquis.

He was peppered with yelled questions that he didn't respond to.

"Did you see who shot Guy Harding?"

"Is it true the sheriff's department thinks you were involved?"

"Did a love quadrangle between you, Loraine Sulley, Drea Dresden, and Guy Harding lead to his death?"

"Is this finally the end for your club?"

The tumult ended as he went through the gold-framed, glass-doored entrance where, very visibly stationed, two black-suited bouncer types stood, ensuring the continued privacy of the hotel's celebrity guests.

He knocked on the bungalow's French doors and a gaunt Duncan let him in. Elvis Costello's "This Year's Girl" was playing on the record player Drea must have brought over.

She and Loraine were curled up at opposite ends of the luxurious white couch, which was almost swallowing them up.

"Beer?" Duncan popped the cap off a bottle of Sol from the bar set up at the far side of the spacious living room and handed it to James.

"Any news?" asked James.

"Well, we aren't watching that shit." Duncan pointed at the big TV, which took up one corner of the room. "The news coverage on TV in this country is so fucked up. It makes me sick what they are saying about all of us."

James, who, other than last night, never watched the news anyway, didn't say anything. He hadn't heard Duncan angry before, though.

"Sorry, James. I'm trying to keep it together but some of the things they are making up are so horrible, and catching Guy's murderer seems to be the least of their concerns.

"Anyway, Suzanne called today and said the law will likely release Guy's body this week so we can make arrangements to fly him home for a proper funeral. I've asked Drea and Loraine to come, and I'd like to extend that invitation to you as well."

"Thank you, Duncan. Thing is, I've got the LAPD and the fucking sheriff's department on my back right now and they wouldn't let me leave town, to use the old cliché. I was torn about asking you right now, but other than the shit that went down with that redneck in Austin, did the band have any other problems or confrontations in the States?"

Duncan sat between the girls and, taking his lead, James plopped into the matching white chair that faced the couch. The freezing-cold beer tasted good.

An unusually quiet Drea got up while Elvis was singing "Little Triggers" and flipped the album over to side two, dropping the arm four songs in to "Living in Paradise," which presumably summed up her feelings.

"Nothing like that really, James. I mean, New York was like LA, or London for that matter. I suppose we were essentially preaching to the converted. Once we got on the road, Drea told us we were going to some off-the-usual English band circuit places, and we gradually realized that our manager had made sure our agents booked us into towns where what we were saying would piss off the locals. So, there was a mix of fans and screaming bottle-throwing anti-fans. We had to get out of a few clubs pretty quickly. Our tour manager was smart

113

enough to mostly book motels on the highways in those areas so they wouldn't follow us back to our rooms, or else we'd sleep on the bus and get dayrooms in the next city. It made for good publicity, of course, especially with the NME writer who came along to send back his impressions to England. There were some close calls but mostly it felt more surreal than anything."

"I can imagine. And nothing too weird since you and Guy have been in LA? Like no dangerous unresolved moments with any drug purveyors Drea might have introduced you to?"

Drea shot him a finger.

"No. One very 'LA' producer pissed us off but he was in more danger than Guy and I," Duncan said with a wistful half smile.

"I don't know what to think, then, Duncan. I promise to do what I can. There's a lot swirling around that doesn't make sense yet."

Drea finished whatever she'd been drinking and leaned into Duncan. "Honey, I need your help with something in the bedroom." She rose and took the guitar player's hand, leading him to the back of the bungalow.

James imagined Loraine knew by now what that meant. When the door closed, he said, "Are you going to go to London?"

"Yes. I think I should. I thought a lot about it. I don't imagine Guy's family will be happy, but I know Duncan will appreciate it, and I have a feeling Drea won't go. Plus, I have to leave the country soon before my visa expires, so it might be best to spend some time in London before I try to get back into the States."

"Are you sure? What about your band? We have dates booked for you, too." James felt bad even as the words left his lips.

"James, I thought about that hard. In truth, it was very tempting to pretend that everything with Guy was just a bad dream that would soon fade. It was just a couple of weeks, right?"

"And what about the other night with us?"

"You tell me. You didn't seem to think it was a good idea at the time."

"Well, on very rare occasions, I'm wrong."

"My mind's made up, James. If you care about me, you know it's safer for me to get away. Tony Marshall scares the hell out of me and knowing he's into some business with a homicide detective is very dangerous information for me to possess, especially living here."

"Alright, girl. I guess you're right. I talked to Patrick Goldstein, the journalist who introduced me to Marshall, and he's trying to help me learn more about what Marshall might be up to. My fucking mind's spinning still from your Holton revelation. I can't get my head around what they could be up to, but the pair are a nasty combo, whichever way you look at it. You're dead certain it was his voice, right?"

She nodded.

He'd decided—for now, at least—not to tell her about the mob connections, which obviously would elevate the fear she was already wracked with.

"Okay. Look, I'll do everything I can to sort all this shit out while you are away. Just be careful in London. If you start meeting people in the ska and reggae scene there, it's possible Marshall could hear about it."

"I will. You be careful, too, James. It's one thing to try to help find out who killed Guy, but those two cops already hate you, so don't start digging into their connections with Tony Marshall. You may be street-smart but that's a whole other world of darkness you're not equipped for."

She came over and kissed him lightly on the lips. "Besides, I might find I miss you while I'm in London."

CHAPTER 23

THE FOLLOWING FRIDAY, A Cadillac stretch limo pulled up at the Pan Am terminal and deposited the four of them curbside, where a pleasant, fresh-faced young publicist who introduced himself as David Millman solicitously got Duncan and Loraine checked in while James and Drea trailed along in their wake. Duncan had spent most of the ride pleading unsuccessfully with Drea to change her mind and let him buy her a ticket.

Nothing further was said until it was time for goodbyes at the gate. "When will I see you again?" said Duncan to Drea.

"Honey. Just come back when you are ready to record some music."

"What the hell are you talking about? You think I'm going to come back to this fucked-up place or ever record again?" snarled Duncan.

"Baby, I just thought since you and Guy had already written more than enough songs for the next album that you would want to…" she trailed off, stoned, confused, and hurt.

James put his hand gently on the guitarist's arm. "Mate, maybe this is way too soon to talk about it, but you're not honoring the dead if you let your dreams end on that sidewalk along with Guy."

"Fuck, James. You too? Does this town make you numb to everything but success? Guy's down in the hold of the plane in a fucking box and you two are talking about the next album? You make me sick."

He grabbed his boarding pass from the now freaked-out publicist and headed to the gate.

They'd ridden to LAX with no music, which was anathema to James, so he quickly remedied that, pushing in the cassette of Roxy Music's first album as soon as the driver closed the door. He and Drea flopped back into the hermetically sealed darkness.

"I gotta ask you, what made you decide not to go to London?" said James as "Ladytron" cast its reflective melancholy spell of romantic manipulation.

She shrugged and fingered one of the bullets in her cross-shouldered belt absently. "Stuff, I guess. I couldn't be fucked to put on an act for his parents or Guy's or anyone else at the funeral, for that matter."

"Was Duncan expecting you to?"

"He didn't say it in so many words but I could tell he was nervous about me."

"Who wouldn't be?" James laughed.

She grinned. "Fuck you. But actually, you wouldn't be nervous because you genuinely don't give a toss what anyone thinks about you or your friends. Maybe that sums up why I'm still here."

Her eyes closed and stayed that way for so long James wondered whether she'd nodded out. "You awake, girl?"

She opened her eyes. "I was six when I saw my dad die. It was on *The Untouchables* when Elliot Ness gunned him down. He was away on location for weeks so I didn't believe my mother when she told me he was alive. He died a lot for the rest of my childhood, on everything from *Gunsmoke* to *Burke's Law* and *Mannix*. I was just thinking that Guy will probably come back soon."

"Look, I know I shouldn't say this, but you sure all this smack is good for you? I mean, look at Darby. It wasn't long ago that he and I were back-to-back, on top of a table at Dani's Oki Dog, throwing shit and fighting it out with some jock punk wannabes. Last couple

117

of times I've run into him, I feel like his spirit's fading away before my eyes."

"Don't knock it until you try it, honey. Why haven't you, anyway? You have to be curious and you don't hold back on anything else. I'll shoot you up now, if you like? My treat."

"If There Is Something" started and gave James a haunting, nostalgic jolt back to London.

"The most perfect double bill of all time for me was Roxy Music with David Bowie and the Spiders from Mars at the Rainbow Theatre. Eighteen hundred kids in their glitter, platform boots, satin and tat, sat in rapt silence, awash in stylized future dreams meshed with deco decadence and romantic longing as their design for living. Being clearly shown how it was possible to dream up your own future if you were brave and imaginative enough. You and I need to keep doing that.

"A friend had told me that earlier that night he was at his dealer's house buying some speed and the dealer offered him smack and said, 'First time's free but after that, you pay, boy, and pay and pay.' That part didn't fit in with my dream. I didn't want anything or anyone controlling me."

"And that's why you won't?"

"Partly. But also I was about fifteen when me, Ross, and a few good mates started, um, experimenting with various things, and I read some stupid newspaper article in the *Daily Express* or some other rag saying smoking cannabis eventually led to shooting heroin. What a ridiculous bunch of shit, but in that moment, I said everything's fair game; however, I'm never sticking a fucking needle in my arm. See, I would just hate to be proof that that self-righteous establishment writer and all the fucked-up schoolteachers were right, ya know?"

"Okay, honey. Fair enough. I know I've asked you a lot to shoot up but I won't again."

"Besides, it's so fucking expensive, and I need records and clothes more."

"Well, it used to be but not lately. That's why I'm making the most of it."

"Really? How come?"

"Some new dealers. They're selling prime, uncut China White. Pure as the driven snow for a tiny fraction of the old prices. I love it."

"How'd you find them?"

"They found us, really. A couple of East LA guys started showing up at the Masque earlier this year and now that they know the punk kids, they tell us when to be at the Canterbury. They take over an empty room, and we all just roll on up. So great."

"Really? Isn't that a bit risky for them doing something so regularly and not controlling the environment? Seems like it would leave them wide open to be robbed or busted sooner or later."

"Huh. I hadn't really thought about it. They are big guys who I imagine are armed, so I can't really see any of the art punks trying to rob them. They seem pretty smart and clearly don't use their own product but they don't seem remotely worried about getting busted either, which is unusual, now that you mention it. It makes it so easy to score, though, and it's clearly good for their business."

"Okay, putting that aside. What are you going to do since you're staying?"

"I don't know for sure. My dad thinks I should go into the family business, as he puts it."

"Acting, huh?"

"It would be good to make some money but I hate most films these days. Everything's gone downhill since all those cool seventies films. I swear, *Jaws* ruined things. You know, I'm like you and mostly watch thirties and forties films these days. Still, I guess you don't have to watch what you are in."

"True. Still, maybe you should try writing. You're the only person I know who reads more than I do."

"Maybe I could. A book would be cool. What about a script?"

"Yeah. You know how films about teens and music always feel completely unauthentic? Do a good one."

"Remember when they kicked us out of the Ramones' Roxy show while they filmed for *Rock 'n' Roll High School* because we wouldn't jump up and down and act like morons? That film was abysmal. I could definitely do better than that."

"You should do it now. It feels to me like the door that opened a crack the Clash and the Pistols kicked wide open is starting to close. I don't want either of us on the wrong side of that door. I'm serious, Drea. We might not get another chance."

"What are you going to do if they shut your club down?"

"I can't let that happen. I'm gonna open tonight. That place is all I have, and I ain't going down easy. The Rebel Rockers are playing. It was in our *LA Weekly* ad last week and they'll have flyered. It should be busy but not enough to bring the fire department down."

The limo dropped off Drea and then James. He listened to his messages, which included Rebel Rockers manager Henry Wrenn-Meleck confirming their load in time and Lou saying she'd handle sound check. But the last one was the most interesting.

"Hi, this is Denise Hamilton from the *LA Times*. My colleague Patrick Goldstein told me what's going on at your club. I've actually been there a lot. It's great. I'd love to talk to you about what you're dealing with."

CHAPTER 24

JAMES HAD KNOWN THAT stepping onto the sidewalk outside the club for the first time since the murder was always going to be surreal, but he'd not been prepared for the chalk outline of Guy's body that kids were standing around or the goth-themed tributes that lay up against the wall, not to mention the bullet holes in the double red doors. Shaken, he focused on lugging his yellow milk crate of records onto the ticket window where Lou was putting a pile of small bills into the till to make change with. He walked 'round the bar and back to her.

"Thanks a lot for handling things that night. It meant a lot. The law doesn't know you saw everything as far as I know, so hopefully no one's gonna be thinking about your legal standing here in LA."

She smiled wanly. "Thanks. I can't get it all out of my head, though. I saw a lot growing up in the east end of London but this was like something out of an old gangster film. Why would they shoot him, of all people? And how come the cops thought you had robbed the place up the hill?"

"I don't know. I'm trying to make sense of it too. Listen, there's a *LA Times* journalist coming down here tonight to talk to me, Denise Hamilton. Let her in and don't charge her if she asks for me, okay? Was sound check alright?"

"Yeah, they were fine. They have a guy with them but you have to find someone reliable for us, James. I don't really know what I'm doing."

"So many of these LA sound guys are bitter, frustrated musicians and irritate the fuck out of me, though, and I think you're doing a great job. But I'll ask around if you want."

He dropped "Money in My Pocket" by Dennis Brown as Lou let the first kids in. He was glad it was the Rebel Rockers tonight. He liked their singer, Princess's, voice. He had huge reservations about white guys with dreadlocks, though, nicknaming them "trustafarians," so he couldn't resist teasing the band's guitarist, Redlocks. The guy was amiable, though, and it should make for an easy night. He was happy to see some Jamaicans trickling in too, one giving him an approving nod as "Jack of My Trade" by Sir Lord Comic boomed through the sound system.

He got lost in it all for a while and felt better than he had for a long time. "Draw Your Brakes" by Scotty was playing an hour later when Lou called out that Denise Hamilton had arrived. She was a cool-looking, tallish woman with dark-red hair cut in a short bob, which went well with her 2 Tone influenced skirt and jacket.

"Thanks for coming down, Denise. Can you give me a few minutes to get the band on stage and we can go back and talk in the office?"

She nodded. He pulled Big Youth's *Dread Locks Dread* album out and dropped the first side on the turntable. He walked down the bar and squeezed past Pilar, who was popping beer bottles at her usual fast pace. He spotted Redlocks coming out of the office.

"Oi, oi, you ready to go on?"

"Jah, man, absolutely. Looking forward, like a stepping razor we dangerous."

James avoided an eye roll and said amiably, "I'll use Peter Tosh as your cue then. Five minutes alright?"

He went into the tiny office comprised of a small. old wooden desk and two chairs that almost filled the room. He'd expected to find it full of smoke, figuring that was why the guitarist had been back there, but although there was a box of matches, no smoke. He picked up the box, which slid open to reveal a small vial of coke. James grinned. *Wow. What an image buster for the ganja-only advocate.* No wonder he'd wanted the office's privacy.

James walked out through the end of the bar and stepped the few feet across to the "dressing room," which was only separated from the Klub-goers by a thick curtain. He stepped in and greeted the band.

"Have a good show, you lot. There's a nice crowd already." He tossed the box of matches in Redlocks's direction. "I think you forgot this, mate."

He thought he saw a blush as he turned and headed back to his turntables and dropped Culture's "Two Sevens Clash."

He saw Denise at the bar talking to a large Mexican guy he'd noticed on the dance floor a few times lately. The guy was a little older than a lot of the kids, and he'd taken it as a compliment that this cat was open to new sounds.

He announced the band over "Stepping Razor" and motioned to Denise to meet him at the end of the bar. They ducked into the office.

"Thanks a lot for coming in to talk, Denise."

"Patrick told me you are having problems, and I was curious to hear more about it, especially as I like what you are up to."

"How'd you get into ska?"

"I'd just left college last year and was on holiday in Europe before I started work at the *Times*. I was on the cross-channel ferry to England from Calais and these boys were trying to chat me up. They claimed they had a big hit song in England. To be honest, I didn't believe them, but it turned out to be Madness and, of course 'One Step Beyond' was indeed a big hit over there. When I heard about the O.N. Klub, I got curious."

"That's brilliant." James laughed, picturing the ferry scene.

"So fill me in on your problems, James, and don't leave anything out."

He ran through everything, from Mata's first visit and the fire department aggravation to the false robbery report and Guy's shooting. He did leave out the Tony Marshall part of the story, though. She prompted him for more detail here and there but mostly just listened, writing on a small spiral notepad until he finished and then she started in.

"I grew up in this neighborhood, which is partly why the Metro editors made this part of my beat at such a 'tender age.' I'm in the midst of a story on the CRASH anti-gang unit for the Rampart Division. Do you know much about it?"

"No, I don't know anything about it. I don't even know what it stands for," he admitted.

"Well, it was started in '73 and was initially called TRASH, as in Total Resources Against Street Hoodlums. But activists claimed defamation against the youths and the LAPD relented and changed it to CRASH. The plan was that every district would have an anti-gang unit and relay information between themselves to help break them up. They have a very gung-ho rep and claims of unlawful arrest, planting of evidence, and police brutality are widespread. I'm sure a lot of those claims are justified. Because I'm local and grew up here, I've been able to get a lot of people in the community to talk honestly and from the heart to me. I'm trying to think if any of your problems could figure in my story but on the surface, they don't.

"I know the shooting happened right after the cops came for you but it's hard to see any potential link to the real estate guy and a gang shooting. At least superficially, the gangs are pretty homophobic. On top of which, this guy's efforts to gentrify the neighborhoods could lead to longtime locals being priced out of their homes, which wouldn't go down well at all."

"Do you know anything about him? I mean, as far as I know, I never met the guy, so to give them my description as an armed robber seems extreme."

"Well, his name's Curtis Manthorne. He presents himself as a real estate agent. In reality, he's buying most of the homes himself though, making some improvements, and then pocketing a tidy profit by selling primarily to the gay and lesbian community as that's where his relationships are. Obviously, it's currently way cheaper to buy here than in Hollywood or anywhere farther west. It's ironic, considering your club is obviously welcoming to any and all, but he may well think the rowdy rep will hurt his gentrification efforts."

"Yeah, Detective Mata alluded to that himself."

"What's your gut with the actual shooting then? Have you had any issues with the gangs, any trouble inside the club?"

"No, none. Honestly, I don't know if any of the kids who come in are in gangs, but the only trouble we've really had in here was caused by English hooligans fresh off the boat."

"Did they attack any Latino kids?"

"They started trouble a couple of times with some mod/ska kids. One of them could have been Latino. I didn't think about it at the time."

"I just had a thought. Ruben, the guy I was talking to at the bar, has been here since he was five, but he's not legal in the US, so the last thing he needs is to get dragged into anything with the authorities. He likes the music here and might talk if I promise him neither of us would go to the cops, linking him with any info he gives us. Will you promise me you'd honor that?"

"Yeah, of course. Ask him to come back here."

Denise slipped out and James stood in the doorway. The Rebel Rockers had the crowd going but their songs of peace and hope didn't diminish the dark thoughts of murder plots and conspiracies that swirled round and round in his head.

Ruben was a bear of a man and the three of them barely fit standing in the tiny office. He and James shook hands but that was the extent of their direct communication, as neither was bilingual.

"I'll ask him if he thinks the gangs have any issues with the club or if he knows anything about the shooting."

She and Ruben went back and forth in rapid-fire Spanish for a couple of minutes.

When they paused, she said, "As far as he knows, you're clean with the gangs, because you haven't copped an attitude with any locals and have comped some underage kids. He hasn't heard of any gangsters claiming the hit on Guy Harding. Personally, he really likes the music here and wants to know more about ska."

Knowing the English and Mexicans shared a love of vintage American cars, James said, "Ask him if he knows of anyone who drives a matte-gray '51 Ford Custom with tinted windows?"

After another exchange, she said, "You hit pay dirt, James. He says it belongs to a couple of guys new to the neighborhood who arrived from Mexico earlier this year. Story is they're selling cut-rate heroin like it's going out of style. The rumors are that they have police protection."

"Fuck me. That sounds like they could well be the guys my friend cops from but I can't see how that could motivate them to a murder." In one of the least English moves of his life, he hugged Ruben. "Mate, thank you so much. If Denise will translate, I'll give you the history of ska over dinner one night."

Denise stayed in reporter mode with another back-and-forth and made notes in English as fast as they talked in Spanish.

"I got their first names—Jesus and Francisco. They live on Hoover, which is very close by. Ruben doesn't know anything else he can think of. Could you ID them if you saw them?"

"No. All I remember is the tinted windows rolled down and two guns blazing, which I guess means there were two shooters and probably a driver in the car. All I can ID is the car."

Ruben was clearly ready to head back to see the band, so James walked out with him and motioned to Pilar to comp his beers.

Back in the office, he asked Denise, "What's the next move? Looks like you just got an exclusive."

"My editor will never go for this. We need more. You've no real proof. You didn't even have the license plate, right? Also, if these guys do have police protection, they may not do a thing if you go to them now. You know you can't put Ruben in the middle of this, right? Everything he said was off the record."

"Yeah, and protecting someone else is why I've held a few things back. I know you can protect your sources as a journalist but if I give you the rest, we gotta have a deal to work together and share information before you print anything. If what's spinning around my head is true, this shit could get us and the people I got to try to protect killed."

"When and if I file a story, it will take on a life of its own. The killing's already started, so why don't you run the rest by me?"

"I need to follow up this lead you just handed me, and I think I know how to do it. I promise you I'll share anything concrete that I find out, okay?"

"You think that's the right thing, James, but it's naive to think you can do this on your own. C'mon, spill. I promise I won't go to my editor without telling you first."

"Okay. This all just hit me and might be a mental mad conspiracy theory, but here's the rest...

"Patrick introduced me to a music biz guy who's deep into the reggae world named Tony Marshall. Come to find out he's connected to the mob and a very violent man. Loraine, the singer from Top Ranking, accidentally overhears him on a call discussing 'upping the shipments.' When he finds out, he threatens to kill her if she ever speaks about it. At the time, I couldn't figure out why he thought that was a dangerous thing for her to know because I figured he was talking about records. The day after the murder, I'm at Rampart and Loraine is waiting in the lobby while I'm getting grilled by Mata, and two sheriff's detectives, who already have a hard-on for me, come walking in, discussing me. She realizes one of them, Johnny Holton, is the guy on the other end of the call with Marshall. I've been racking my brain ever since as to what their connection could be, but when Ruben said our dope-dealing, possible shooters had police protection, it all came together. What if Marshall, with his mob connections, is supplying the heroin to Holton and that's what they were discussing on the call?"

"That's a huge what-if, James."

CHAPTER 25

THE NEXT MORNING, A blazing-hot shower in his beautiful red deco-tiled bathroom kicked in the beginnings of a plan, albeit a stupidly dangerous one. He called Drea.

"You were right. It's time I bought some heroin."

"Honey, are you sure? After all you said, I think I might feel guilty now."

"I said buy but I'm not intending to try it. There's a good chance that your dealers are also the ones who shot Guy." She gasped and he filled her in on last night.

"Why do you want to buy heroin from them?"

"I can check if the Ford Custom driven by the shooters is parked near the Canterbury to make sure it's the same guys and maybe we can learn something when we are doing the buy."

"Like what? You can't exactly ask if they are looked after by a maverick detective or do some part-time hits."

"Yeah, I know it's risky but I'm thinking if I go in, all disarming London boy, maybe I'll learn something. I just thought—did you ever bring Guy and Duncan with you?"

"No. I always go on my own. Come to think of it, they only let one person in at a time, so this isn't going to work. Anyway, if they did kill Guy and two of the people there that night come waltzing in together, it might totally spook them."

"Well, yeah, I'd figured I'd gauge their reaction."

"What if their reaction is to kill us too?"

"They aren't going to shoot us at the Canterbury with a bunch of punks hanging out waiting to cop. Anyway, I'm thinking about asking my Irish mate Norman to come as backup."

"Well, if you are right and they are essentially working for the cops, why wouldn't they? There wouldn't exactly be a public uproar if a couple of kids died at the 'notorious punk apartments,' ya know. When I hear they are coming, why don't you get Norman to drive us up there? I'll go in and you two can drive the block and see if the car's there. These guys are used to seeing me and will be less suspicious if I probe a bit."

"I dunno, Drea. I want to get a read on them, and I don't feel good about you going in alone now."

"Honey, you being there will only risk it becoming more dangerous. Did it ever cross your mind they were shooting at you? You and Guy are both skinny Englishmen. Think about it. If they are working for that cop who hates you, it would make a lot more sense. Why would they want Guy dead?"

"Yeah, you're right. Fuck. Sometimes none of this shit seems real."

"I know. I just said you and Guy are English. I can't get used to talking about Guy in the past tense. Sometimes, at night, in bed, I just pretend he went back to England so I don't have to think about it. I wonder if that's partly why we didn't go to the funeral."

"Maybe. I know I said everything is changing but I hadn't figured on anyone dying, at least not like this. Alright, let's do this your way, but be careful. I know we probably need to do more than ID the car to get Mata to do anything but at least it would be a start."

⊚⊚⊚

DREA GOT THE WORD Wednesday. James called the glass-cutting and installing company that Norman worked at in North Hollywood and filled him in. An hour later, after making up some bullshit reason he had to leave work, the Belfast man was at James's front door.

Norman drove them south on Havenhurst, which turned into Kilkea once they crossed Willoughby. She was outside her place waiting and was sporting the rapier she'd been carrying that day at the Sunset Tower, which seemed like a lifetime ago to James. He noticed that the dried blood was still on the tip.

"You planning on taking that in with you, girl?" asked James.

"Maybe." She grinned. "Or perhaps I'll leave it with you two buccaneers in case you need to rescue me."

Norman pulled a pint bottle of whisky out of the glovebox on the side with the missing front seat, took a swig, and handed it back to Drea over his shoulder.

"Good to meet you, Drea. Here's some Dutch courage, although, from what James tells me about you, I'm guessing you don't need it."

She swigged it, happy at the implied compliment, especially as it wasn't something James had ever said to her face.

Norman had Van Morrison's "Blue Money" playing as he took Beverly east to Highland and then north through the pleasant, well-maintained homes that gradually transitioned to grimy car repair joints, dingy bars, and the like as they passed Melrose, heading up toward Hollywood Boulevard. He hung a right onto Yucca.

As they stopped to turn onto Cherokee, James said, "We'll drop you out front and go look for the car, then wait outside for you. How long do you think?"

"Maybe ten, fifteen minutes depending on how many people are looking to score too." She jumped out curb side without another word.

Norman glanced at the dilapidated building. "What a shithole, guv'nor."

"Squire, you don't know the half of it until you go inside. Why don't you drive slowly 'round the block and let's see if these fuckers are the ones with the Ford Custom."

They drove slowly back up Cherokee, passing a variety of beat-up old cars but all way more recent in vintage. As soon as they turned right onto Yucca, though, there it was—three cars in on the right, tightly tucked between a pale-blue Dodge Polara and a rusty gold Pontiac Firebird.

"Fuck. That's it," said James.

Norman pulled alongside. "That was easy. They weren't trying to hide it, were they? What now?"

"It makes sense. They have no reason to hide it. Let me get out and get the license plate. The cars are too close to see it from here."

Norman gave him a pen and pad he used for measuring jobs. James climbed out of the Bug, leaned between the Pontiac and the Ford Custom, and scrawled it down. He couldn't see anything inside with the heavily tinted windows but as he turned to get back in, the driver door swung out and slammed into him from behind, knocking him headfirst toward the VW.

A stocky guy with black cropped hair and an oversized white Dodgers T-shirt came flying out of the car and stood over James. "What the fuck do you think you're doing, *puto*?"

"Ease up, mate. I love old American cars and had never seen this model before. I just wanted to write it down," James ad-libbed.

The London accent paused the guy long enough for Norman to get out and join the conversation.

"That's right, man. Don't get your knickers in a twist."

It was likely this guy had never heard that expression before but the mocking tone and expression would have filled him in if there was any doubt in his mind as to its meaning. He looked more than ready and capable of having at it with both of them but was maybe weighing the advisability of a fight given his presumed role today.

He stared Norman down for a full minute. "Get the fuck out of here before I take you both out."

Norman returned the death stare.

"Alright, squire. Time to go," said James.

The guy leaned back against his car as they climbed back in Norman's VW.

As they drove off, James looked out the back window at the driver and suddenly saw Drea flanked by two guys with their arms around her, half carrying her down the block toward the car. One of them was carrying an incongruous black briefcase. Even from this distance, James could tell she was fucked up.

"Fuck. Fuck. Norman, reverse back. These cunts have got Drea."

The Irishman slammed the car into reverse but as they got near the Ford Custom, a red Chevy pickup truck barreled down Yucca toward them. Norman slammed on the brakes.

The Chevy driver was leaning on his horn and screaming out his window at them. Norman pulled forward and U-turned on a dime, which on a VW Bug was London cab level good.

As they swung back west on Yucca and dangerously U-turned back east, he could see the dealers had hauled Drea to the Ford Custom and James could hear them as Norman pulled over.

The driver was yelling. "What the fuck is going on, Francisco?"

"This bitch started asking questions, and I think I saw her outside the club that Saturday night. I dosed her for free so we can get her somewhere private and find out what the fuck she knows."

They threw her in the back as Norman pulled up alongside.

James jumped out and ran toward the car as the doors closed. He grabbed the passenger door handle but the car screeched out, leaving him on the sidewalk. He ran back and jumped in the VW. "We gotta stay on them, Norman. They'll kill Drea once they get what they want out of her. I know it."

CHAPTER 26

BOTH CARS FLEW DOWN Yucca, which weaved its way toward Vine.

"Squire, if they get onto a freeway, we'll never catch them. There's an on-ramp north of here on Vine. We have to get to them before then."

Norman slammed Frankie Miller's *The Rock* cassette in and the title track blasted out at full volume.

"Don't be so sure of that. No one's outrunning me, especially if my man Frankie's on."

The Ford hung a fast left on Vine as the light turned red. Traffic started flowing north, blocking them, but Norman eased through the red light and forced his way onto Vine. The Ford was already blocks ahead, though. They passed Hollywood Boulevard and a few cars turned right, allowing them to get closer. But James could tell there was no way they could catch up if these fuckers took the freeway east. Norman was singing along with "The Rock" at the top of his voice and, despite his immediate fears, it crossed James's mind that this guy could have been a good soul singer.

The Ford slipped into the lane for making right turns east onto the freeway. Norman yelled "hang on" and slammed into and up the curb onto the sidewalk, scattering the few pedestrians in his path. He was now alongside the Ford as it neared the on-ramp. James could see his grin in the rearview mirror. As the Ford came onto the off-ramp, Norman floored the Bug and it hit the right wheel and fender of the

Ford, which spun back left and flew up the curb, hitting the wall on the other side of the on-ramp, before rebounding into the rear end of a parked blue '72 Pinto, which instantly burst into flames that threatened to also engulf the ruined classic car. Norman steered the Bug past the wall, then back onto the road, pulling over in a red zone up the block.

James got out and looked back. The smoke and the tinted windows meant he couldn't see what shape the occupants of the Ford were in but a clearly stoned Drea stumbled out on the passenger side.

As they got out, James saw the rapier and grabbed it, not that he'd ever used one before.

Norman flew out, and they both ran toward the Ford. Francisco clambered out the same door Drea had exited from, with his gun drawn on her.

James realized he'd never get there in time. At the top of his lungs, he yelled, "Drea, catch it," and threw the rapier high and toward her.

She looked at him as it arced her way, clearly disoriented. Her right arm shot up, though, and in the most epic, elegantly wasted move of all time, caught it, bringing it down in one fluid motion, slicing the right side of Francisco's cheek wide open. As blood gushed, she cut open a three-inch-long flap on his left cheek. He dropped the gun, which landed on the floor of the Ford, and fell to his knees, screaming in agony as James and Norman got there.

Norman pulled open the driver's side door but the guy was out cold. The passenger, presumably Jesus, hadn't fared as well. Blood poured from his busted-up face, which had clearly smashed into the windshield on impact with the wall. Neither were wearing seatbelts.

Francisco was screaming "You fucking bitch!" at Drea.

He saw Norman looming over him. "Help me. She attacked me."

James smiled to himself, realizing this idiot thought Norman was a random passerby. Norman obliged and lifted him to his feet.

"Thank you. Can you get me to a doctor before I bleed to death? I'm in agony," said Francisco.

"Just call me Dr. Feelgood," said Norman, before hauling back and punching him square on the jaw.

Francisco hit the deck, lights out.

"I'm gonna go call Mata. Got to get to him before some random cop shows up. Let's leave the gun. We don't want any of our prints on it. Are you okay, girl?" said James.

Drea gave him a loopy grin and nodded as she surveyed her handiwork.

He saw a payphone up the block on the other side of Vine and sprinted up there.

A few cars slowed as they passed by but no one bothered to stop. He pulled Mata's card out of his wallet, deposited dimes, and dialed. He got through to the detectives line, identified himself, and asked for Mata, who came on a minute later.

"Listen, Detective. I found the shooters who were driving the Ford Custom that night. You need to get here fast. They're in the vehicle at Vine by the 101 on-ramp east, north of Hollywood Boulevard."

"You don't say, Dual. Have you asked them nicely to wait for me?"

"Well, actually, they are currently incapacitated after an accident, but they could come to any time. You can't miss them. They hit a blue '72 Pinto, which of course exploded. I can't fucking believe they still allow those death traps on the road."

"That's outside our jurisdiction, strictly speaking, and what the fuck have you been up to now?"

"Are you kidding me? Seems to me like I've been doing your job for you and I'm calling you so you can take credit 'cause maybe—just maybe—I trust you'll do the right thing, Detective. These fuckers live right near the club, as far as I can tell, which is in your jurisdiction, right?"

"Okay. I'll send a car over. We can always say we followed them, but you'd better be right about all this. Don't leave the scene. I want you down here pronto to give me the whole story."

James ran across the street and back to the car where Norman stood watching while Drea thrust and parried at no one in particular, obviously well pleased with herself.

"The law's on the way. We don't have much time. I want to trust Mata but it might be safer if you took Drea back to my place. We don't

135

need her getting pegged by the law as a drug fiend, and you're likely over the alcohol limit. She seems okay but more fucked up than I've ever seen her. I'm not sure how much of that shit they gave her, so stay with her for a bit if you can and make sure she stays awake."

He pulled his house keys out and handed them over. "You okay to wait with her until I get sorted? Sorry about work."

Norman nodded. "I've no love for the law, so fine by me if you're sure. But let me check on our friends first."

The Pinto was still burning but the fire hadn't spread to the Ford Custom.

Jesus looked in a really bad way but it was hard to tell with the driver. Norman lifted his head off the wheel and slammed it back onto the wheel. He got no verbal reaction. He then poked Francisco in the ribs with his work boots and heard a slight groan, so booted the guy hard in the head, which ended the groaning. He walked over and took Drea's free hand.

"I'll take you to James's home, Drea, and maybe you'll tell me how you acquired those skills."

She acquiesced and James smiled at the odd couple as they walked up to the VW and climbed in. They were barely out of sight when two black-and-whites screeched up behind him and two cops jumped out of each, guns drawn.

"Hands in the air!" yelled a blond crew-cut identikit LAPD member, his quasi-Aryan/Nazi vibe present and correct.

James complied. "Hey, I'm James Dual. I called this in to Detective Mata."

A similar-looking cop went behind James, pulled his hands behind him, and cuffed them. "In the car, punk. We'll sort this out when we get you all down to the station."

They threw him in the back of one of the black-and-whites, shut the door, and started inspecting the prone Mexicans. The window was cracked, so he could hear their observations.

"Looks like a single-car accident. The Pinto must have been parked. The doors are locked and no one would have done that if their car was on fire. Ford driver's out cold. No visible bleeding, but serious-looking contusions on the forehead."

"Passenger in the front looks seriously fucked up. Guess we can't drag him in like this. If he croaks we'll have the fucking NAACP all over us again. Better call for an ambulance and a fire truck."

James could see them leaning over to get a closer look at Francisco now. "This fucker looks like he's been in a knife fight or some shit. Weird."

The blond Nazi poked Francisco a few times with his boot, which elicited a new round of groans.

He and the look-alike hauled him up, cuffed him, and tossed him in next to James while Francisco started cursing and ranting in Spanish.

"Shit, there's a Magnum .45 on the floor in the back. Let's call in for an investigation unit. This doesn't track as a straight-up car accident."

They got to work, pulling out some barriers and placing them around the car. The two Nazis got in the front of the black-and-white James was in. The others stayed at the scene, presumably to secure the integrity of the scene or, of course, do whatever seemed expeditious for their needs.

They read James and Francisco their rights and pulled onto the off-ramp, which was still operating freely with the Ford all the way onto the sidewalk. Without any obvious inconvenience and minimal pedestrians, no one had bothered to stop. Cops rousting Mexicans for no apparent reason was an everyday occurrence.

CHAPTER 27

As they arrived on Temple at the Rampart Division entrance, James kept his mouth shut but was furiously working up a story he could try to sell to Mata without involving the names of anyone he needed to protect. Francisco had been giving him death looks all the way, muttering what were doubtless threats in Spanish.

They were led to the check-in desk. The usual bustle of sad activity was all around them, albeit slightly less on a Wednesday afternoon than his Saturday late-night visit. He buried the wave of depression that hit him.

Nazi One spoke to the rotund gray-haired cop at the desk, who had a pleasing gruff/grizzled forties-era vibe.

James clicked back into his preferred noir fantasy mindset.

"Hey, Charlie, book the beaner on a possession of an illegal firearm charge for now while we see what else we can nail him for. Mata wants to talk to the limey before we book him."

"I'd watch that beaner talk around Mata."

The Nazi rolled his racist eyes and led James down a now-familiar corridor and pushed him into yet another interview room without bothering to uncuff him. He was left for what felt like a very long time before the door finally opened and Mata entered.

"This how you treat concerned citizens who are trying to help and support the law?"

Mata almost grinned. "You sure as hell aren't a citizen and trying to involve yourself in an active criminal investigation could cost you that green card you somehow managed to acquire, not to mention your freedom. You beginning to get the picture, kid? Stay the hell out of Rampart business in the future."

"Alright, Franc. I get it. Is the lecture over? You want what I got or not?"

"You'd better give everything you got, otherwise you'll be booked on the same charges we're working up for your friends in the Ford Custom with. Funny—you seem to be the only one not injured in the 'accident,' huh?"

"You mind uncuffing me first, Franc? I've received your message, okay?"

Mata stepped to the door and ushered the Nazi in, who duly set his hands free. "I can handle this one on my own, Officer."

The door closed, and they were alone again.

"I already know you're not going to like most of this, and I can't prove much, so try not to lose it with me over what I tell you, okay?"

No response as Mata leaned back in his metal chair.

James, elbows on the interview desk, leaned forward, aiming for a picture of complete candor. "So I'm on my way to the club with a mate and we see the Ford Custom coming down Hoover toward Sunset. That gunmetal, halfway through a respray look, and the tinted windows were a dead giveaway. We follow it into Hollywood, where it pulls up outside the Canterbury Apartments, which houses half the punks in LA. Two of the three guys you now have get out and go in. The Ford drives 'round the corner and parks. I wait a bit and then go in.

"I ask some random kids there and story is these two are openly dealing dope and that they apparently have police protection. I go back to the car and when they exit, we follow them as I want to see if they go back to Hoover before I contact you. My mate, not being experienced at tail jobs, probably follows a bit too close. I'm figuring they remember we were behind them on the way over and get spooked.

"They blast up Vine, trying to lose us, and take the turn onto the on-ramp too fast, spin out and go into the wall, which bangs them all up pretty good. Since they are all out cold and my mate was only supposed to be off work for an hour or two to help me with moving some stuff 'round at the club, I told him I'd call in the accident."

Mata shook his head in disgust. "I don't know whether to laugh at how dumb you must think I am or let the two officers who brought you in give you the same treatment they doled out to your friend Francisco just now. While I decide, explain why you called me if you believe reputed drug dealers have LAPD protection. Surely I'd just turn them loose, right?"

"If you didn't like the first bit, you're gonna hate the rest. First off, though. You're a fucking hard-ass and as much as I wanna hate your guts for a lot of the shit that's happened at my club, I think, in your own way, you are not only honest but believe you are doing the right thing for your neighborhood.

"All I wanted to do was have a club that was open to anyone, play forward-thinking, positive music, but somebody got murdered outside of it and I have to get to the bottom of why.

"If you trust me at least as much as I'm trying to trust you, maybe we can sort all this tangled web of shit out. I'm not trying to insult your intelligence but I'm also not willing to put at risk more people who are completely innocent bystanders just to fill in how I learned what I have.

"So now it's conspiracy theory time. Nothing made sense until I found out the shooters are drug dealers, too. I can't prove any of this but I believe Sheriff's Detective Johnny Holton and maybe his partner are getting major quantities of dope from a New York crime family via a mobbed-up music businessman, Tony Marshall."

Mata closed his eyes and rubbed his fingers on either side of his forehead while he absorbed this and weighed up what tack to take now. "Okay, Dual. You're right—ID'ing the car but not the occupants isn't enough to charge them with murder. You didn't get the license plate the night of the killing and even if it's the same car, you can't ID anyone to prove these guys were in the car that night. You are lucky in that we found a briefcase full of smack along with a Magnum .45 in the car, so that part of your theory checks out.

"We can run ballistics on the gun to try to match the ones dug out of Guy Harding but I highly doubt they would be dumb enough to still have those weapons. There were two guns used in the killing, as two different kinds of bullets were found in him and the doors and wall of your joint. Two of the guys are in the hospital under guard and will be charged and moved to the county jail's hospital when they regain consciousness.

"Since it's just the two of us talking and I'm almost willing to believe that in your own fucked-up, half-assed, dumb way, you are trying to help, I'll tell you this much. I know you like your noir shit, so you are probably aware that historically there's no love lost between the sheriff's department and the LAPD. Given there's no cooperation usually, something smelled wrong when those two were so hell-bent on helping me nail you. I'm not saying I buy what you are selling me just yet, but I think you believe it. If you want to go any further, though, you are going to have to name names, give me dates, times, and places where any meetings or conversations you are aware of took place."

"Thank you, Detective. I understand. Can I sleep on it? Um, preferably at home and not here?"

Mata finally grinned despite himself. "Maybe, if you admit your story about today is half-truth and half made-up shit created not to involve people you like. I'm going to need the truth before this goes to trial."

"Fair enough. If I can sleep on that, too, I'd truly appreciate it."

"Just this once, since we have these guys cold anyway. Let me ask you, though. One of your friends, the driver perhaps—he a big Irishman? Also, our friend Francisco told some wild story about a gringa bitch with a sword who went Errol Flynn on him. She ring any bells for you?"

It was James's turn to grin. "Wow. That's hard to imagine, huh? Think he was dipping into his own product?" He got up to leave. "Any chance of a ride home this time?"

Mata rose, too, and pointed to the door. "Sure. Why don't you ask the nice patrolman outside? He's all through with Francisco for now. You two could shoot the shit on the way home."

"Skip it. I'll call you Thursday."

He reached out a hand to Mata, who shook his head. "I don't like you that well yet."

142

CHAPTER 28

JAMES RANG HIS OWN doorbell but wondered whether anyone would notice, as even through the solid adobe walls and three-inch-thick wooden door, he could hear Iggy Pop's "Five Foot One" blasting out. A well-oiled Norman opened it a minute later.

"Guv'nor. You're home. Drea and I are having a wee dance. Have a Bell's." He handed James a half-empty fifth of their favorite Scotch.

More than ready, James grabbed a glass from the kitchen and poured himself a tall glass almost full, with a tiny amount of water on top.

Drea came over with a complicit, happy grin of the highest order and gave him a full bore hug. "I got that motherfucker good, huh?" she said in an elegant but nasty tone, extending the word for several seconds.

"Yes, girl, you absolutely did. A moment of true perfection. Francisco's still talking about it, probably. Not that the cops really give a shit, fortunately for us."

"Really? You sorted things out? Well, you must have if they let you loose." She laughed throatily.

James wondered whether Norman had got Drea dancing to avoid her nodding out permanently but felt relieved and, in the moment, found the elation infectious. By the time Iggy started "I'm Bored," they all sang every line with gleeful venom.

Norman raised his glass. "Here's to dollface and the chairman of the bored."

"And to the squire," said Drea.

"Yeah, it does feel good but we have to get our stories straight before I get too wasted.

"I skated today because they found a briefcase full of smack and Francisco's Magnum but Mata will want a truer version than the bullshit one I made up before this goes to trial. Although we somehow managed to get Guy's killers arrested, it's not on murder charges yet. They are running ballistics on the weapon but it's a long shot. With you, squire, my only concern was if they'd tried to bust you for drunk driving and clearly that can't happen now. I told them we'd just seen the car on the street and followed them after you'd taken time off work to help me with some shit at the club and I left Drea out entirely. I can't tell them about Denise's friend Ruben, so I think we have to stick to that part if possible. It's trickier with you, Drea. Obviously, I didn't want them to go after you on heroin charges or peg you for a junkie and fuck with you in the future."

"Well, if you had to, you could say I was with you and say I went in to scope things out as I know people there and they grabbed me and shot me up, which is true."

"Shit, sorry. What did happen, anyway? How did they get suspicious?"

"I tried doing the LA girl version of your idea. It wasn't hard. You get told so many times growing up that men like ditzy women with high-pitched voices. It's always made me sick but I know how to do it—or at least thought I did. I was just like, 'All your dope's so great and cheap. Where does it come from, and I love coming here to get it and see my friends at the same time. You guys are so nice to bring it here. How come you don't make us go to dangerous places like all the other dealers who'd be too paranoid to deal this openly?' I probably went too far when I nudged Jesus and said, 'Is someone big protecting you?'"

"Fuck, Drea. I can't believe I let this happen to you."

Even as fucked up as she still was, she sharply corrected him. "I went in because I wanted to get those fuckers just like you do, okay? Anyway, they started talking in Spanish and before I knew it, they'd grabbed me. Francisco held me down on the floor, arms splayed, and Jesus shot me up in the arm with the biggest load.

"I was rushing like crazy but scared. They marched me out. I don't remember who was in the lobby but I don't think anyone said anything to them. I was fucked up but the fear kicked my adrenaline through the roof like I'd had speed, too. The rest you know."

"Okay, we could tell Mata what happened, leaving out your prior smack habits, and he'd also then have them on kidnapping charges. On the other hand, if I can avoid involving you…it's hard to imagine any lawyer they might get thinking it's a good idea to bring up this Errol Flynn mystery gringa bitch's attack given the additional charges that would likely follow if it all came out. What do you want me to do, Drea?"

"Errol Flynn gringa bitch, huh? I like that. I want you to get on with that Scotch and flip the album over."

He got up to do as requested. "Okay, I'm on it." He downed the Scotch and started pouring another from the ever-shrinking amount. "I hope there's another one?"

"This is going to be a heavy session. Better call Bogie's Liquor to deliver a couple more bottles," said Norman.

"Good idea. Is your motor banged up? In all the excitement, I didn't notice," said James.

"Not too bad, man. The front left-side panel's dented but I know a panel beater who'll do it cheap. It's not the first time."

"Way you drive, I'm not surprised to hear that. Seriously, though, I'll chip in to pay for it as long as the club manages to stay open this weekend."

As he went to dial, he thought of Denise Hamilton and realized he owed her an update.

After placing the Scotch order, he left a message for her at the *LA Times* city desk.

CHAPTER 29

JAMES WOKE FROM A fitful sleep with traces of a surreal nightmare where he had vainly tried to save Sue Ann and Guy's lives.

Drea was still out but breathing normally.

He'd been nervous about her during the night and hadn't slept much, not knowing how long heroin really lingered or how the large quantities of Scotch that followed it might affect things. But it appeared her constitution must be on a Keith Richards level.

Norman, who had crashed on the couch, had apparently rolled off to work at some stage of the now-departed morning. James's place looked a total mess and smelled like a bar: albums all over the place, in and out of their sleeves, along with a couple of packed ashtrays, empty glasses, bottles, and other detritus. He opened the big bay window that faced onto Fountain and then headed for a long shower.

As the intense jet hit the back of his neck, he wondered how the fuck he'd managed without this in the bath-only culture of England all those years. It really worked today and his mind started whirring. He dried, got half dressed, checked on Drea, who was still sleeping, and headed to the kitchen. He started prepping the old Italian Bialetti stovetop espresso pot and dialed Suzanne Black in New York. Her assistant put her on after a brief hold.

"Why, hello, James. Are you calling to hear about the funeral? I just got back last night."

"Um, to be honest, Duncan got pretty upset with Drea and me at LAX, and I haven't heard from either him or Loraine about when it was going to be, or anything else for that matter."

"Yes. David, my West Coast publicist, couldn't help but overhear that exchange."

"Sorry. Anyway, I'm sure it must have been rough. How are you feeling?"

She sighed. "I'm okay. The funeral was held on the family estate in Sawbridgeworth, Hertfordshire. It was a mixture of the anticipated upper crust but the parents were very generous in that they allowed the band to invite friends of Guy's. I'm sure they would have ordinarily found them all highly inappropriate. The senior UK label people were there but as the band hadn't really broken in the US yet, no one much from New York bothered to go. To be honest, I was relieved they weren't there as most of them would have been an utter embarrassment.

"The press were kept out entirely but my London counterpart arranged for a couple of tasteful shots to be released. There were a lot of fans but as surreal as they all looked in that country environment, they just left wreaths at the gates. The family crypt is on the estate so it will never be like Jim Morrison's Pere Lachaise ongoing circus, mercifully."

"I have some news to share, too. Long story short, it's pretty certain we found Guy's killers yesterday. They are in police custody on a bunch of heavy-duty charges but there's not enough evidence to nail them for the murder yet. The press don't have anything, but a journalist is helping me, so that may not last long depending what her editor thinks. I think my next step may be to come to New York, but I need to talk to Loraine first. Can you help make that happen?"

"Yes, of course, but this is a lot to take in, James. My head's spinning. How did you find the killers and what's with needing to come to New York? Not that it wouldn't be nice to see you."

"I promise to fill you in in person, but I have to talk to Loraine first. She may be in danger and I need her blessing to enact what I have in mind. Do you know where she's staying?"

"I believe she and Duncan are still in the countryside. What do you mean, 'danger,' though?"

"I trust you but I don't want to say any more until I've spoken to her, okay?"

"Echhh. I can't stand secrets but okay."

"Suzanne, c'mon. Your line of work means keeping all kinds of secrets, I bet."

"Okay, I can't stand not knowing a secret might be more to the point."

"Can you ask Loraine to call me urgently? It's about one p.m. here, so only nine p.m. in England. I'll wait at my place for a few hours."

"Okay. When are you thinking to come to New York? Do you have somewhere to stay?"

"Well, I stayed at the Chelsea Hotel the first time I went in '77 but post-Sid and Nancy and all that, it feels like a vaguely depressing idea. If I can pull things together, I'd like to head in after Saturday's show so I can get back for the following weekend's gigs at my club."

"Well, everyone should stay at the Plaza at least once. We get a rate there, and I'll set you up."

"Thanks. That's really cool of you."

"No problem. I'll take you to some fun places if you'd like, as a counterpoint to whatever dark deeds you are planning."

He smiled broadly. "Dark deeds, huh? Yeah, that's spot-on. It'll be great to see you."

"Until then, James." She hung up.

He vividly felt the finger that she'd pressed into his palm along with her business card that night at the Roxy. It felt like a lifetime ago and for Guy, of course, it was.

His phone rang an hour later. "James? It's Loraine."

"It's good to hear your voice. How are you? Do you have privacy so we can really talk?"

"You have no idea. This place is like something from another time. There's rooms for everything. I'm in the telephone room. There's servants everywhere, and they are all white, so you can imagine the attitude they are giving a Jamaican girl. Honestly, though, in some ways, it's been good to be here. Guy's parents have been pleasant to me although they haven't actually acknowledged that we were lovers. It was a beautiful ceremony and being here instead of hiding out in LA made it real and final."

"In England, living in denial and not expressing emotion is *de rigueur*, but I'm glad it feels like you made the right choice. I like to think I left all that repression behind but maybe I was continuing it by not being at the funeral myself. Anyway, I need to run a few things by you so we can agree on the next steps."

"What do you mean, we?"

"You gave me some advice before you left and wise as it was, I don't think I can follow it, so I want to talk to you before I make any more moves."

"Okay. Fill me in."

"I've been digging around, partly with the help of a *LA Times* journalist. We found out who owned the car the shooters were driving. It turned out they are the heroin dealers Drea's been buying from at the Canterbury. Drea, my mate Norman, and I went there when Drea knew they'd be there selling. The plan we had to find out more went sideways, and they dosed Drea and tried to kidnap her. We chased them and Norman ran them off the road. We had a near miss but got lucky and the three of them are in police custody for dealing and weapons. They don't have enough to charge them with Guy's murder yet but there's no doubt in my mind they did it."

After a pause, she said, "So you think it was all connected to Drea buying drugs from them? Had Guy met them?"

"No, he never met them, and I don't see any motive for killing Guy. You're not going to like this but here's what I think. The guy who told the *LA Times* journalist Denise Hamilton and me who they were also said they had police protection, which made sense considering how brazen they were. Ever since you told me that Detective Johnny Holton was the one on the phone with Tony Marshall, I couldn't figure out why. I also found out from Patrick Goldstein that Marshall's likely partner in the music publishing business is Paul Castellano, head of the Gambino New York crime family, who, among other things, is big in the heroin business. I think the call you overheard was Holton asking Tony to up the heroin shipments. That's why Tony was so flipped out.

"Hate to say it but what if the shooters were told to hit you and possibly me? Marshall waited until he was three thousand miles away and then decided to erase any possibility you heard everything or maybe told me. Also, as much as Holton and his partner Fred Ostrow already hated me, if the heroin connection's real, them showing up at Rampart that day would make a lot more sense. They likely wanted to make sure I didn't know or spill anything about Marshall's drug business once they found out Guy was the one who ended up dead."

"This nightmare keeps getting worse, James, but at least they got the murderers. Do you think the police will get them to talk?"

"I doubt it. They are running ballistics on the gun that was in their car but it's a big, long shot. The only real way to end this is to bring Marshall and those fucking cops down. The killers probably don't even know about Marshall and will be way too scared of Holton to talk about him. I believe Mata, although an asshole, is honest. Thing is, to get him to go after Holton, I'm going to have to tell him about you overhearing the call. I've kept your name out of every conversation I've had with him but he won't do anything without some hard facts to go on. Can I get your permission to do that? If I can, then I'm thinking to go to New York and try to see Marshall. Tell him I'm sorry about what happened with you but that I'd still like to do business with him. I think it might put his mind at ease and make him think that we don't know anything. You know, tell him you might come around if we negotiate a better deal for you or something like that. It should buy some time free from him trying to clip either of us and maybe I can learn more about what he's up to."

"Are you completely crazy? I told you not to go digging. You are way out of your depth. I don't ever want to see him again. He's already in my nightmares. I was too humiliated to tell even you but when he picked me up and shook me, I was so scared I wet myself. He saw urine running down my leg, James. You have any idea how soul destroying that is? He had this cold smile like he enjoyed that a lot."

"Fuck, girl. I'm truly sorry for everything you've gone through but if we don't do something, this will always be hanging over us. It's no way to live."

"Alright, James. Do what you have to with the cops and tell Tony Marshall what you need to, but promise me I never have to be in a room with him again, okay?"

"Okay, thanks. Can you stay in the country a bit longer? It might be better not to go back to London until I take care of this."

"Maybe. It's going to feel awkward soon, though. Duncan's talking about going back at the weekend."

"How is he?"

"Drinking heavily and not great. Maybe it'll help if I tell him the cops have the killers."

"Yeah, I hope so. It's best you don't tell him the rest. I'm going to be on the move a lot. Give me the number there and can you let Suzanne know how to reach you if you leave? I promise you I'll be careful and hopefully I'll see you soon."

As he hung up, he turned and saw Drea curled on the couch. "You're awake. Good. How much of that did you hear?"

"Enough. You really like her, huh? You know, you may be onto something with that Paul Castellano mob meets music business theory. Stevie Marriott told Ross the night we were all at the Speakeasy in London that he was threatened by Castellano and John Gotti when he went looking for all his unpaid Humble Pie royalties. He never received a dime, apparently."

CHAPTER 30

MATA SHOWED UP FIFTEEN minutes late at Lucy's El Adobe on Melrose across from Paramount Studios, by which time James had already ordered a Sol beer. Mata slid into the small brown leather booth in the low-key, white-brick-walled but frequently celebrity-riddled joint.

"'Ello, Franc. I haven't been here before but given this place's celebrity rep and the Governor Jerry Brown and Linda Ronstadt of it all, I'm surprised you picked it."

"Like most things, kid, you don't get it. Lucy's good people. Apart from keeping this place going ever since it opened in '64, she founded the Mexican American Political Association. Later, after *LA Times* journalist Ruben Salazar was killed by the police while covering an East LA protest in 1970, her husband Frank scrawled Salazar's name in wet concrete outside here as you'll see when you leave, if you open your fucking eyes."

"Interesting. Surprised you're not trying to close her down, too."

"Very funny, smart-ass. That was actually partly why I became a cop."

"Can you tell me a bit more, Detective?"

"If you're really interested, the LAPD has targeted people in my community for generations, not to mention the government heavily drafted us for the war in Vietnam. I'd been thinking about joining but the outcome of those protests sealed it for me. So after ten years on the force, when you tell me some white cops are drafting young men into the heroin trade, I may not want to believe you but I'm not naive enough to think I can just ignore it."

"That's actually very reassuring as I'm about to trust you with things that could shorten the life expectancy of me and my friends."

A smiling woman with a strong, angular face, her black hair cut page-boy short, dropped menus on the table and leaned down to hug the cop. "Franc, my boy. How are you? It's been too long. Now you are a hotshot detective, you too important to come and see me?"

"Never, Lucy. It feels like a twenty-four-hour-a-day-job sometimes. Plus, on top of it, I now have this kid causing me trouble."

She looked at James. "You look like a nice boy. Franc's a good man. You'd best listen to him, okay?"

"I'm trying."

"Now, what shall we feed you two today?"

"I'm still discovering Mexican food," said James.

"Well, I'm from El Paso, Texas, but the first thing you need to learn is that there's not one food that's Mexican. Every region has its own unique dishes and often ingredients. Let me think. For you, the mole poblano. Franc, I'm guessing the chile verde?"

Franc nodded a smile, and she bustled off, a swirl of color in her floral dress. "So what have you got for me?" said the cop.

"First off, the Irish guy is my mate Norman Lynas and the gringa bitch is a friend, Drea Dresden...yeah, the actor's daughter. The boys you have in custody got suspicious and grabbed her. So if you want, you can add kidnapping to the charges. They will both make statements when you need them to."

"I hate to tell you but it's a boy we have in custody, not boys."

"For fuck's sake. Tell me they didn't get bailed out?"

"The two in the hospital were both found with their throats slit this morning."

"You're fucking kidding me. How could that happen? Surely you had them under guard?"

"Yep. Guards outside all night, apparently. Seems like the killer or killers got in through open windows from outside the hospital building. An investigation is underway."

"Wow, your boys royally fucked up, Franc. You want me to trust you with my friends' safety when this sort of shit goes down on your watch?"

"Not my boys. They were taken to the Hollywood Community hospital, a small one-hundred-room facility with no security to speak of on De Longpre, which is outside our jurisdiction—as was the accident site, you may remember. Strictly speaking, we should have turned Francisco over to the Hollywood division, too."

"From the sound of it, it's lucky you didn't, although being in county jail's not exactly safe for him, with the Sheriff's running it, is it?"

The cop was spared needing to defend the jail conditions by a young waiter who arrived with their dishes, along with a red plastic mesh basket loaded with warm corn tortillas.

Mata dived straight into his, which James eyed a bit enviously being a pork lover but only until he tasted the mole poblano, which was like nothing he'd ever tasted before but liked instantly.

"So what else have you got for me?" said Mata.

"You don't exactly put me at ease, given what you just told me."

"Look. I warned you the first time we met. Maybe you should have gotten out of the club business if you can't handle what can come with it."

"Point taken. Okay. So here's the full story with Tony Marshall.

"He's big in the reggae world, has been for a long time and over lunch says he can help me get some bigger artists from that world in my club. But in exchange, he wants me to help sign Loraine Sully, Top Ranking's singer, to his management company. Now, despite the fact that on the way to our lunch I witness him smash a baseball bat over a receptionist's desk up on the Strip while demanding money for some unpaid debt, I still stupidly set up a meeting. Loraine goes over to his suite at the Beverly Hills Hotel, where he's lounging around in a robe, clearly aiming to consummate the deal in more ways than one.

"During said meeting, he gets a call and, wanting privacy, tells her to hang up when he picks up on the bedroom extension. She overhears who she now is certain was Holton asking Marshall to 'up the shipments.' He comes out in a rage, claiming she listened in on the whole call. He shakes her in the air while making it clear she's dead if she's lying. She's petrified but we go and meet one more time and tell him she's not signing the contract, which also took her publishing rights. He makes thinly veiled threats if the deal's not signed before he leaves town.

"Then Guy's shot while we were all standing outside the club. The next day, Loraine's in the Rampart reception while I'm in seeing you when Holton and his partner come in, ranting about me, and she's stone-cold certain he was the one on that call. I'm now thinking Marshall likely ordered the hit and that they were aiming at Loraine and possibly me as we were standing next to Guy Harding."

Mata, who had been eating in a manner that suggested his chile verde was more interesting than the story, looked up and chewed meditatively before waving his fork in James's direction. "Well, you're right about one thing. You were an idiot to send her to this clown in the first place if even a trace of your tale is accurate. Secondly, you've got zero that would hold up in court."

"Yeah, I figured. Thing is, I hear Marshall's tied in with Gambino crime family boss Paul Castellano. Could you at least check that out? If that family is in the heroin business, it might make sense that Marshall, who's in and out of LA for music business reasons, could be a low-key go-between and potential bagman, right?"

"It's a big reach but I will. I don't know what good you think it'll do though—you still got no proof."

"If it is true, can't you lean on Francisco and find out who his source is?"

"So you're okay with police brutality just so long as it's not aimed at your limey ass?"

"Well, they are killers and I hate what heroin's doing to people in the punk world. He would have shot Drea without a second thought that day too."

"Well, let's just say we have thoroughly discussed things with him already and got nothing. Tell you what. I'm going to be receiving shots of his two partners with their throats slit later and perhaps that will help loosen his tongue. I'll offer to put him in solitary and discuss a little plea bargaining with a side dish of witness protection program. You got any more bright ideas?"

"I do but let me ask you something first. That fucking real estate guy's still in the back of my mind. I don't see him as part of this, and I've not had time to really check him out amongst all this shit. Why would he risk making a false report that could have got me killed?"

"Since it's just you and me right now, I'll tell you unofficially what I think. I did a bit of checking, not because I give a shit about you particularly of course, but he's a bit more than just a real estate agent. He's making lowball offers to local families who are having trouble with their mortgage payments. Then he makes minor improvements and sells quickly at a fat profit, mostly to people from the gay community because that's where his relationships are. Seems like he's pretty overextended and needs to sell that place above your club as quickly as possible. With all that noise and street traffic, hundreds of extra cars every weekend, maybe no one wants to buy that headache. Perhaps he just couldn't wait for us to close your doors for good and tried to speed things up. With you out of the way…bingo."

"What a fucking asshole. I should go and fucking have at him."

"Settle down, killer. Listen, unofficially, I don't like what this opportunist is up to, but you need to stay clean here. Plus, there's no way he would have been involved with our shooters. There have been a number of attacks on men leaving gay bars. The gay community is convinced they are perpetrated by gang members. There's sadly a lot of mistrust on both sides, so no way a gay guy is going to hire our suspects. I'm talking to the El Centro del Pueblo community center to try to find ways to alleviate the situation. Now let's hear your bright idea."

"Well, Franc, you impress me more and more. I can imagine that you aren't getting much support from your cop colleagues. Anyway, my idea's another dumb, risky one. I'm going to go see Marshall in New York. Tell him I'd like to patch things up so we can still work together. Maybe I can buy some time so he doesn't make any more attempts to off Loraine and perhaps get some proof about his ties to Holton."

"For once, you are right. That is dumb and risky but I guess if it blows up on you, I'd at least be rid of you. Maybe I should talk to NYPD and get you wired up for the meet. It sounds like he's overconfident and reckless if he took you to that stunt he pulled on the Strip. You might get him to incriminate himself."

"As good as that sounds, Franc, thanks, but no thanks. We don't know who we can trust, New York cops included if the mob's involved. I'm going to leave after this weekend's gigs at the club. Any chance you and the fire department could leave us alone so I can focus on New York?"

"That might be arrangeable. Maybe if we give you a few more weeks, the asshole above you will go under. Just promise to turn kids away once it's full and get some kind of food in there before our truce ends so the underage kids are legal to walk through the door, okay?"

"Fair enough. You know, this might be the beginning of a beautiful relationship, Detective."

"Don't get carried away, kid. You're no Rick Blaine. Your dump's no Cafe Americain, and I'm no womanizing Frenchie."

CHAPTER 31

ON SATURDAY, AFTER ARRANGING a meeting with Sugar Hill Records owner Sylvia Robinson, he called the number on Tony Marshall's card, which turned out to be to his club. After a couple of minutes on hold, he was put through.

"Englishman. This is quite a surprise."

James wondered whether the surprise was largely because Marshall had hoped he'd be dead by now.

"Yeah, Tony. Honestly, I feel badly how things ended at lunch that day. I know you could have done a lot for Loraine, and I think we would have done some good business together with other Jamaican artists. I'm coming to New York Sunday to meet Sylvia Robinson to see about doing something with Sugar Hill at the club, and I thought maybe we could get together and see if we can find a way for me to make amends and to put that behind us."

"Possibly. I hope you are bringing your girl with you?"

James ignored the inference this time. "Nah. I want to look into some other artist bookings while I'm there, so better to be on my own."

"Well, it's going to be a busy week. Bob's playing Madison Square Garden, as you probably know."

"No, I didn't, actually."

"He's playing two nights with the Commodores, which will give him an opportunity in front of a predominantly black audience for the

158

first time in America. I'll arrange a pair of tickets for you and will see if I can carve out some time so we can discuss what the future might look like, if there is one for you and me. Where are you staying?"

"The Plaza."

"Business must still be good at your club. I'll call you with a time and place."

As ominous and risky as that felt, James said, "Thanks, Tony. I really appreciate it."

"By the way, are you meeting with Sylvia Robinson's partner too?"

"What—her husband?"

"I was referring to Morris Levy."

"Who's he?"

"Oh, Englishman. You are too funny. How are you surviving?"

The line clicked and went dead.

James called Patrick Goldstein and brought him up to date on everything that had happened since their pie à la mode and then asked about Morris Levy.

"Gee. This whole New York idea sounds extremely high-risk for you and low hope of getting Marshall to admit anything that will tie him to bent cops, heroin, and murder...unless, like some noir story, he reveals all before he offs you."

"I know but by going there and just talking music business, even if I don't get any hard proof, I'm hoping it will convince him that Loraine and I don't know anything about all that. Staying here like a potential sitting duck and having her paralyzed by fear of him is no way for either of us to live. We'd always be wondering about when the next 'drive-by' or whatever attempt is going to happen."

"It's your funeral, as they say. Talking of funerals. Morris Levy. It would take hours, if not days, to tell you what I've heard over the years. In a business riddled with outrageous, larger-than-life rogues and pirates, he is truly the kingpin and probably the most feared by other record men along with any artist who has had the serious misfortune to attract his attention. I don't know how Sylvia got into bed with him but I'm guessing it's via her somewhat disreputable husband Joe.

159

"Morris started a club, Birdland, in 1949 and soon moved into publishing and then a label, Roulette Records. In 1956, he released a lot of great rock and roll records while allegedly never paying any of the artists royalties. He's extremely aggressive about adding his name to writing credits on songs like Frankie Lymon and the Teenagers' 'Why Do Fools Fall In Love' despite never writing any song ever. His propensity for violent solutions to perceived problems has led to other label heads walking away when he 'claims' an artist they all want to sign. Tommy James and the Shondells being a notorious example. He also has deep ties to the Genovese crime family."

"Wait—is he the guy who sued John Lennon a few years ago for using a line from a Chuck Berry song in 'Come Together'?"

"Yep. He forced Lennon to record three songs he published for the Phil Spector-produced Lennon album *Rock 'n' Roll* and when the album wasn't completed due to problems with Spector, Levy released Lennon's demos on a mail-order record."

Despite himself, James laughed at the brazen moves. "Should be an interesting trip."

"If you survive it."

James threw a few things into a travel bag. As requested, Yellow Cab driver Lenny arrived a couple of hours earlier than usual so James could do a bit of crucial shopping before the club opened.

They drove down to Melrose Avenue first to cool boutique Cowboys and Poodles that had a nice mix of new and vintage clothes, but James struck out this time. He jaywalked to the south side of the street to Let It Rock, where owner Alan Jones stood under the white façade, trying to fix the flickering pink musical note neon that overlaid the black logo. James had loved the sax man's ex-band the Amen Corner as a kid, so he liked buying clothes here, not to mention he'd bought from the original London Kings Road shop and appreciated a vague bit of continuity in his surreal world. Alan took him in the back to where a new shipment had just come in, but the London store, clearly deciding all Americans were big, had neglected to send any jackets or boots James's size. Alan put out a couple of lines by way of consolation.

He and Lenny dropped down to West Third and zipped into Strait Jacket, where Genny Schorr hooked him up with a cool, long, black jacket and some tasty pointed-toe Chelsea boots. He'd seen her band, Backstage Pass, open for Elvis Costello at the Whisky in his early LA days and loved what she'd conjured up with the boutique. Then east into Hollywood, first to a SaveMart store, which he'd chosen solely because Don Adams of sixties spy spoof TV series *Get Smart* glory was their TV pitchman these days, but they didn't have what he wanted. A detour up sharply rising Laurel Canyon took them to Pacific Stereo, where he bought Sony's recent brilliant invention the Walkman Cassette player, which felt invaluable for the five-hour-plus New York flight. At $200, the cool blue and silver device had actually cost more than the flight but felt worth it. Mission accomplished, they cut back down the windy Laurel Canyon and headed west on Sunset to Tower Records.

Lenny pulled into their lot, which, being a Saturday, was full and double-parked while James zipped into the brightly lit, cavernous store. He moved quickly through the crowded aisles that felt more like a supermarket than a traditional small record store, finding cassettes for exactly the New York soundtrack he needed.

He dropped cash and carried his swag out in the trademark yellow plastic bag with red Tower logo and jumped back in the matching Yellow Cab. As they headed east on Sunset toward the club at the other end, he said, "Thanks for the runaround, Lenny. Any chance you can take me out to LAX when I'm ready to leave the club?"

"Sure, James. Where you headed?"

"New York. You used to have a cab back there, right? How long is it since you were there?"

"About four years. You think LA's crazy. New York's a cesspool, I'm telling ya."

"Mate, that would have been 1976, the year Martin Scorsese's *Taxi Driver* came out, right? What happened? You see that and worried it could be you if you stayed any longer?"

"Yeah, something like that."

Lenny left it at that and James didn't press. They made it to the club shortly after opening time, and James hurriedly lugged the milk crate of his records for the night out. "You want to hang out here until it's time to go?"

"Nah. Can't afford to. I'll pick up some rides but don't worry. I'll be back in time to get you out to LAX."

CHAPTER 32

TONIGHT HAD ORIGINALLY BEEN booked and advertised as a Top Ranking show but the eager Untouchables had agreed to fill in. There were already a few people inside, so he quickly found Clyde, who was leaning against the bar with the rest of the band. Unlike the other bands, rather than sit in the dressing room, the Untouchables still liked to dance before their own set, being the core regulars they were.

"Hi, James. This is a first. No records to start the night?"

"I know. Listen, I have to go to New York tonight and I need to leave a bit early to make the red-eye. After your second set, would you spin records until closing? You're the only person I'd trust to do this, mate."

"Wow. Yes. I'd be honored."

"Brilliant. Want to come back now and I'll show you how to work the turntables?"

They headed behind the bar and back to the turntables as Louise gave him a look while she took money from a steady flow of people who were entering into silence.

James dropped a 12-inch of Clint Eastwood and General Saint's "Another One Bites the Dust." He showed Clyde the fairly simple fade control to make smooth transitions between tracks and how to use the headphones to cue up the next song, in this case the English Beat's "Ranking Full Stop."

"You'll do fine. Just promise me not to sneak in too many mod revival bands, alright?"

Clyde grinned.

"Thanks again. Louise will settle up with you guys after. Now, listen, both of you. I've been with the law again today and I'm pretty sure they will leave us alone tonight. I know this isn't the coolest thing to ask, Clyde, but before you finish your first set, can you beg the crowd not to pour out onto the street or drink outside? I'll say something before you go on, too."

"Okay, we'll try but I don't know if they'll listen."

"Louise, you remember that Rasta guy who was here a couple of months ago who wanted to sell Ital food here? I know I wasn't into it but that detective made it a condition of our truce to get food in and this might be an easy way to do it."

"I don't remember his name but if I see him or any of the guys he comes in with, I'll ask, okay?" said Louise.

"Thanks, Lou. I really appreciate everything. Sorry to ask you to settle up with the band again but I gotta go to New York. I'm hoping once I'm back we can try to end all the major problems."

"It's okay with these guys but you know how some managers are, so don't make it a regular thing."

"I should be back before next Friday, anyway, but if not, call Clyde to come DJ."

An hour or so later, James got on the mike but left the mostly instrumental track "Soul Finger" by the Bar-Kays playing.

"Oi, oi. So most of you have experienced the shit we've had from the law and the fucking fire department. Some of you told me this place is important and like home to you. So if we are going to keep this going, I gotta ask you not to go outside until you're ready to go home. Also, although of course I had no idea, but apparently a lot of you have fake IDs."

This got a big laugh from well over half the packed room.

"So if you have one, please don't buy drinks or at least make sure the fucking picture on the ID is yours."

More laughter.

"Anyway, I know you were expecting Top Ranking tonight but they can't be here so hoping you won't mind too much if the Untouchables play again. You lot ready?"

A nice roar from the crowd as the band made their way on stage.

Once they were on, James went outside to head off any potential trickle of overheated punters.

A few minutes later, a Rolls-Royce Silver Shadow with right-hand drive glided up and a tall, hard, pock-faced man with short black hair, sporting an expensive brown silk suit and shirt matched with leather sandals, stepped out of the rear passenger door.

"This your joint, man?" he asked in a heavy Jamaican accent.

"Yeah. Who are you?"

"Don Taylor."

Fuck, thought James. *Bob Marley's previous and longtime manager.* He'd been the one who took six bullets meant for Marley in the 1976 Kingston assassination attempt but had also been beaten by Marley and others on more than one occasion over money disputes, the most recent of which had, according to Patrick, led to Marshall's reemergence in Marley's life.

"James Dual. What brings you here?"

"I came to see Top Ranking."

"Mate, I'm really sorry. They had to cancel. There's been a lot of shit going on here lately one way and another."

"So I've wasted a night of my limited time in Los Angeles?"

"Look, if you wanna come in anyway, I'd like to buy you a beer. There's a young band playing that are still way raw but promising if you want to check them out. Or, if you like, we can go sit in my office and talk about Top Ranking."

Taylor acquiesced and James led him through the packed throng, acquiring beers from Pilar as they maneuvered a bit of room to lean against the bar.

After a couple of songs, including "I Spy for the FBI," Taylor said, "Where's your office?"

James got two more beers and led the way.

Surveying the grimy office and Taylor's suit, James hesitated to suggest sitting on the equally grimy chairs, but the Jamaican took the lead. Then he pulled out a vial of coke and an ornate silver spoon, proceeding to pack both nostrils before offering the same to James.

"Man, this place looks straight out of Kingston. The band is promising but need a lot of work. You know there was a Jamaican band with that name, too, right? Anyway, tell me about Top Ranking. I hear the singer is a potential star."

"They are pretty raw, too, but I think both these bands are great. They're perfect for this place, anyway. I'm curious how you heard about Top Ranking as they haven't recorded anything yet."

"A boy whom we both know told me that rasclat Tony Marshall tried to sign her and she blew him off. Is that true?"

"Um, something along those lines, yeah."

"Well, I like the sound of that girl already, then. And if she's really that good, showing Marshall what he missed out on would be a nice fat bonus."

"You aren't a fan of his, I take it?"

"I think he poisoned Bob Marley against me. He had a promotor tell Bob I held back money from a concert deposit when in truth it was a deposit for my other client, Jimmy Cliff. Me, who took six bullets for him."

He stood angrily, pulling his silk shirt up, and showed James the crisscross of healed bullet holes and surgery scars that ran across one side of his body.

"It's not me taking money from those who feed me. You know what I hear Mr. Tony Marshall's doing now? Taking the millions mobster Paul Castellano's giving him to buy property in Jamaica to develop as resorts and just leasing the properties while pocketing ninety percent of the money and living like a king. What do you think of that?"

CHAPTER 33

THE PAN AM RED-EYE arrived at JFK around 10:00 a.m. local time. James had not slept despite having drunk copious amounts of Scotch in a vain attempt to override the charlie in his system.

On the upside, he was well buzzed and feeling the added instant adrenaline of being in New York. He had no checked baggage, so made his way as quickly as possible through the drab walkways and escalators that took him down to the street level. Suzanne, having decided to spare James any unwanted gypsy cab adventures through the boroughs, had arranged for a car, the driver of which was holding up a sign with his name on it. Louie, who was squat and one of those guys who, no matter how much he shaved, perpetually looked like he needed one, led him to a black Lincoln town car. The autumn sun was crisp and the air less humid than on James's first visit. This likely meant that the sweat rings under the arms of Louie's worn suit were not recent.

James excitedly pulled the Sony Walkman out of his black leather travel bag and banged in the New York mixtape he'd made. Louie told him he'd seen a wreck on the expressway on the way out so they were going to take surface streets, which was fine by James.

As the Ramones' "I Wanna Be Sedated" segued into the Velvet Underground's "White Light White Heat" and then Bowie and the Spiders From Mars' "Queen Bitch," he felt adrenalized and ready for whatever the city chose to dish out.

They slowly crept through Queens, eventually taking the Manhattan Bridge. As they finally made it to lower Broadway, Television's *Marquee Moon* gave him flashbacks of half-remembered, all-night punk party insanity in an abandoned building lit by bonfires in the neighborhood on his first visit. It took forever to crawl up Sixth Avenue but he enjoyed watching the gradual transitions and shifting cast of street characters work their hustles as they headed up to Midtown. By the time they got to the Plaza at Fifty-Eighth and Fifth Avenue, the sixteen-mile drive had taken ninety minutes.

He gave Louie a tip and took his time walking through the lobby and the highly tempting Oak Bar he could see just beyond. The immaculately dressed, black-suited receptionist found his reservation. But when James reached for the cash in his wallet, the guy told him the room was prepaid and handed him two messages in small Plaza envelopes.

He declined help to the room and stepped into an elevator as Audrey Hepburn and a loud, talky guy he didn't recognize—although it might have been director Peter Bogdanovich—stepped out. His tenth-floor room had a stunning view of Central Park, and he loved the illusion that he was in a film. What kind it was hard to tell, although he remembered the opening scene of Alfred Hitchcock's *North By Northwest* was set here. He tossed his travel bag onto the luxurious-looking bed and stripped before stepping into the beautiful ornate shower, which blasted the red-eye flight's grime and haze out of sight.

Once out, he ordered breakfast from room service and opened the message envelopes.

The first was from Suzanne Black, which asked him to call if he'd like to have dinner later. The second was from Sylvia Robinson, saying that she would spare him the trip out to Sugar Hill's Englewood New Jersey office Monday if he could meet at 5:00 p.m. today at the Roulette Records offices on East Forty-First Street in Manhattan. *Perfect.*

He called Suzanne, and they arranged to meet for dinner near her West Village home. He asked if they could stop by Caffe Reggio, which he'd wanted to visit ever since that great scene in *Shaft* where he bottles the mobster while posing as a bartender. She acquiesced while laughing and told him her flat was just around the corner from there.

He decided to walk to Roulette. He asked Ed the doorman to point him in the right direction. When he heard the English accent, Ed told him he'd been nineteen when the Beatles had stayed here on their first crazy trip, when screaming girls overran the Plaza while police on horseback tried to control things. With that image reminding him of more innocent times, James headed off for the twenty-plus block walk, but not before slipping the addictive Walkman on and starting Isaac Hayes's perfect *Shaft* soundtrack.

The Roulette office was a noisy hive of activity. He waited on a couch in the reception for a few minutes next to a guy who looked like a musician, but James didn't recognize him. They were both led down a narrow corridor by the receptionist, who was dressed very conservatively by typical label standards. She pointed the guy to an office, saying, "Mr. Levy is waiting for you."

Then she directed James to one directly opposite, which contained two modestly sized, worn-looking beige couches. Sylvia Robinson was seated on one, leafing through a big stack of papers in a manila folder. She wore a red leather jacket with a blue turtleneck sweater and black peaked cap. Her black hair was braided into a long ponytail.

She rose with a big smile. "Good to meet you, James. How are you finding New York so far?"

"Just like I pictured it."

"You and Stevie Wonder, huh?"

"Sorry, I couldn't resist. I just got here but the energy of the streets…the whole city…it's like nobody's business, right?"

"Well, as you know, the energy around Sugar Hill is definitely that right now. What got you into our music?"

"It felt like the same burst of rebellion that punk had at the beginning for me."

The conversation in the opposite office was getting heated. James looked right and could see a large man, with shortish black

169

hair combed across to avoid the balding section, seated behind a big wooden desk. He wore a gray suit with an open-collared white shirt. The guy, presumably Levy, had a graveled, menacing voice beyond anything James had heard before, including in any crime film.

"You want fucking royalties, go to England."

"Morris, I just want what's coming to me. We had a big record and I've seen nothing. Write me a check," said the guy from reception, who puffed intensely on his cigarette.

Levy said, "Okay, I'll give you what you deserve," and reached into his desk drawer, pulling out a hefty revolver. To James's horror, he then leveled it at the guy and calmly squeezed the trigger. A bullet crashed into the wall directly above the guy's unflinching head.

In a moment of transcendent cool, the guy said, "Nice shot, Mr. Levy. Now can I have my check, please?"

Levy laughed and reopened the desk, this time pulling out a large binder and writing a check with a flourish. "I like you. Maybe you're okay. Go write another fucking hit."

The musician rose and took the proffered check, quickly glancing down at it. "Thanks, but this don't hardly seem anything like enough."

Levy fingered the gun that lay on the desk. "Don't make me regret my kindness. Now get the fuck out of here."

The guy looked at the check in his hand and, deciding discretion may be the better part of valor, exited, giving Sylvia a rueful look as he turned back down the corridor.

Levy, presumably noticing for the first time that there had been witnesses to the transaction, called out, "Hey, Sylvia. Who you got in there?"

She rose and jerked her head to James to do likewise, and they entered Levy's office.

"This is James Dual. He's got a club in LA and wants to do a Sugar Hill night with us."

"Oh, yeah. That could be good. We haven't done any shows there yet. How long have you been doing this? Is it successful?" said Levy.

"This is the first year, and yeah, we are doing great. Too well, I suppose, as the law and fire department come calling a lot."

"I started out with a club, too, you know. Birdland. Did ASCAP show up with their hand out yet, too?"

"Funny you should mention. Some straight-looking guy shows up one afternoon, saying I had to pay them as we were playing records. I figured it was some shakedown. I told him unless he could show me how any of the artists whose music I played would ever see a penny to get the fuck out. I had no idea ASCAP stood for the American Society of Composers, Authors, and Publishers, though, and thought it was a con."

"Yeah, I thought the same thing but I did a lot of research when they came after me and realized publishing is where the money's at, so I started a publishing company to get copyrights of songs played in my club. Unlike mouthy artists, copyrights don't talk back. You need to wise up while things are hot," said Levy, almost paternally.

"So, James, when are you looking to do this and how do you picture it?" said Sylvia.

"Well, usually I do one artist a night, who perform two sets. I play ska, soul, and reggae records in between but as this music's so new, I thought a double bill...maybe Grandmaster Flash and the Furious Five and Funky Four Plus One or with Spoonie Gee. The Sequence could be good, too, and I'll spin all your other records in between."

"Not the Sugarhill Gang? That's been our biggest hit so far," said Sylvia.

"Yeah, I know. I just think the others might work better with the crowd that comes down," James said, for once diplomatic. "Rapper's Delight" had always felt like a novelty hit to him.

"Never turn down a hit artist. Anyway, since there's no national tour planned, are you ready to fly everyone out and what kind of an offer are you going to make us?" said Morris.

"Mate, I do a 60/40 split of the door in your favor, and you get all this West Coast attention. It'll be great promotion for Sugarhill. I don't have the money to be flying people out."

"You got some balls, kid, coming in here, feeding us that kind of offer. You don't think I could call Elmer and Mario and be in the Whisky or the Roxy in a heartbeat with guarantees?" said Morris.

"Moishe. Give him a break. He's just starting out. I checked things out before I agreed to meet him. The O.N. Klub's got street credibility and it might be the best venue to play to the most diverse crowd," said Sylvia.

Levy sighed and studied James for a minute. "Tell you what, Dual. Maybe what you need is an investor. Someone like me who can make the most out of your club while it's hot. I like that that ska thing's coming back. You know, I cowrote 'My Boy Lollipop' back in the fifties under an assumed name and made a bundle when Millie Small had a hit with her cover version in '64. We can set up a publishing company and get the new bands you book to sign up."

Sylvia shot James a quick, wide-eyed warning shake of her head while Levy continued.

"We can work out a deal, and I'll make all your bullshit problems with the LAPD, the fire department, and whoever the fuck else disappear overnight. It'll be fun for you. How's that sound?"

"Well, Morris, I like the total creative freedom I have and, to be honest, I don't own the lease on the building."

"Listen, if I decide to do this, believe me—whoever has the lease will be more than happy to sign it over to me. And I don't give a shit about your creative freedom. Why do you think that's on the wall?" Levy pointed to a cheesy faux religious scripted framed motto, "Oh, Lord, Give Me a Bastard with Talent," that sat alongside gold- and platinum-framed records featuring the likes of Tommy James and the Shondells, and Frankie Lymon and the Teenagers.

"I help people make the most of their talent, right, Sylvia?"

"Sure you do, Moishe."

"How long are you here for, Dual?"

"I'm going to see Bob Marley and meet with Tony Marshall. Maybe two more days."

"Okay, well, you decide whether you want to make the most of what you have with a proper investor, get a Sugarhill package show delivered. Or, if you want to be small time, we'll just send you home with a box of records to play at your joint and you'll have the law up your ass for the rest of your days."

Levy stepped out from behind his desk and put his arm around James's shoulder while steering him out of the office.

"Better watch out. Tony Marshall's a bad boy. You'd be much better off with me. You know he's connected to organized crime figure Paul Castellano in a marriage I have a feeling is going to go south, especially now I hear rumors he's a go-between for the Genovese heroin business. Shocking to think such people could be involved in the music business, which I've always maintained has no criminal associations whatsoever."

CHAPTER 34

As James walked back into his hotel room, the phone started to ring.

"Englishman, welcome to New York. With Bob's first show tomorrow night, I have very limited time to see you, but a small window just opened. Be at my place at the Dakota at nine p.m. It's apartment number 44. This will be your one chance so don't be late." *Click.*

Fuck, thought James. He'd planned on making their meeting in a public place and didn't like the ominous sound of "one chance."

He called Suzanne.

"I have to go and meet Tony Marshall at nine p.m. now. Are you okay to have a late dinner? Or if you want to come to the Bob Marley and the Wailers show with me we could have dinner there first?"

"The Marley show sounds great. I'll make us a reservation at this new place, Odeon.

"I'm going to drop by Hurrah's tonight to see a band their booker Ruth Polsky says I can't miss and then maybe Danceteria later. Come and find me if you want."

"I'll try. I'm going to Marshall's place at the Dakota, apartment forty-four."

"Why are you telling me exactly where? Is everything okay?"

"I hope so. Just know that's where I went if you don't hear from me. Have you heard from Loraine? She said she'd let you know if she moved from Guy's family home."

"No, but I'll call there and check. Seriously, what's going on? You sound odd."

"I promise I'll fill you in over dinner at this Odeon place, 'kay?"

He pulled on his favorite black drainpipe Fiorucci jeans with the zippered back pockets, along with the sharp new black jacket and Chelsea boots he'd picked up in LA at Strait Jacket.

He took the elevator down to the lobby and headed for the Oak Bar. He was asked to show his room key before they served him the cliched but great Manhattan he ordered along with a dozen oysters on the half shell.

He consumed the reviving combination while reflecting that Morris Levy had likely confirmed his theory about Marshall and the smack, which felt good but undoubtably upped the dangerous nature of his visit. He put his room number on the check, signed it, and headed out, so preoccupied that he almost bumped straight into Andy Warhol.

The porters were unloading bags from a cab, which he claimed for the short ride around the park to the Dakota, figuring things were dangerous enough without walking through Central Park at night solo.

The Dakota loomed in the dark; its Gothic turrets, high gables, terra-cotta spandrels, and oil-burning lamps lent an eerie, haunting feeling to the night.

Once admitted to the building by the white-gloved doorman at the corner entrance that accessed Marshall's fourth-floor apartment, he realized the inner courtyard was so big residents could drive into it. He felt edgy and for once wondered whether he was out of his depth.

As he stepped out of the ornate elevator, a cocker spaniel flew past him, toward the open stairwell.

"You. Catch my dog," said a husky, unmistakable voice.

He moved quickly and managed to scoop the spaniel into his arms before the miscreant could disappear into the darkness.

He turned back to look at Lauren Bacall, his ultimate noir dream woman, which, although an unparalleled surprise, felt strangely natural. He could hardly believe it but she was wearing a houndstooth jacket not a million miles from the one she sported in *The Big Sleep*.

"Thanks. You have good timing and reflexes," she drawled as she took her dog from his arms. "I owe you one. We'd just been out for a walk and she bolted when I took her leash off. What are you doing here, anyway?"

"I have a meeting with Tony Marshall."

"Hmm, you don't fit the usual profile of my next-door neighbor's visitors. You friends?"

"No. We have some things to sort out." James looked around him. "Is there more than one entrance to these places?"

"Think you might need to make a quick exit? I know all those back alley moves, you know."

"I hope not, but I wouldn't rule it out."

"Really? You begin to interest me, vaguely. I know Mr. Marshall is a club owner but judging by his insalubrious visitors who come and go at all hours of the night, I can see where a quick exit might be a good idea. Are you here to kill him, by any chance? I'm not sure how the co-op board of directors approved him in the first place and I wouldn't be sorry if you were, as I'm sick of the noise from his apartment. Although you don't look like a hit man," she drawled in that dusky signature voice that was undiminished by time.

"No, but I do want to know potential escape routes in case our meeting doesn't go well."

"Too bad. The only entrance is the front door. I'll keep an ear open for gunshots. Let me know if things get out of hand. I could use some excitement. It's been rather dull around here lately." She then turned and sashayed back through her open front door.

He rang the buzzer and the door was answered by a hulk of a man dressed in a sharkskin suit. He proceeded to pat James down before wordlessly leading him down a long, wood-paneled hallway that was adorned by various expensive-looking paintings in ornate frames.

They passed four rooms on each side before entering the last one on the right, which could best be described as a library. There were floor-to-ceiling shelves of books on one wall. Marshall was seated on a long, vintage brown leather couch and motioned James to sit on an identical one that faced it.

Behind him, the lead-paneled windows looked out on a moonlit Central Park. "Alfio, go fix us some drinks. I'll have a Bacardi and Coke. James?"

"Scotch and water."

Alfio exited, closing the thick paneled door behind him.

James, feeling all along that an innocent attitude was the best course, said, "Good to see you, Tony, but what's with the pat down?"

"That's standard, Englishman. First off, after the assassination attempt on Bob in 1976, security is always heightened around him and, by extension these days, me. We are going to talk frankly tonight, so in that spirit I also check that people I sit with aren't wearing a wire."

James felt relief that he'd not let Mata talk him into getting wired up by the NYPD. "Mate, I'm coming to you to make things right with us, so why the fuck would I wear a wire?"

"Why, indeed. Perhaps you looked into my background a little. Perhaps you know things about me you think you could turn to your advantage, which would be a dangerous supposition." He spread his arms wide and the fingers on his giant hands that had held Loraine in the air splayed wide. "There are many possible reasons."

Alfio returned, carrying a tray holding their drinks, and placed it on the long ornate wooden coffee table that was positioned between the facing couches and once again exited wordlessly.

"Look, Tony. My club's doing great, other than grief from the law that is essentially a by-product of the success. What I still need to grow further, though—and I know you could help me with—is getting the right Jamaican artists in there. That's my reason for coming all the way here to make things right. Okay?"

"Other than the fact that your reckless, naive approach to the nightclub business amuses me somewhat, what would my motivation be? I don't own a piece of your club and you utterly failed to deliver what I asked for, which I believe you sabotaged deliberately." Marshall leaned forward and raised the tall glass of rum to his lips, taking a long swallow.

James did the same with his Scotch to give himself a moment to think. He knew the key was to make Marshall feel unthreatened by anything he and Loraine knew.

"Yeah, look. Honestly, I'm sorry about bringing up the publishing part of the deal, but any lawyer she might have gone to would have done the same. As I get to know her more, I think I did you a favor. She's very stubborn and wouldn't have been willing to fire her band. You're better off without her."

"We may have a different approach to women, but I can assure you that once signed, the last thing that little girl will be with me is difficult," Marshall said coldly.

"I'm going to tell you exactly what's going to happen to make things right with us, but on the off chance you truly don't know anything about me, here it is. My partner in the publishing company is Paul Castellano, who is head of the Gambino crime family. That's right, I'm a mobster. And unlike most people, I make no secret of it. It's a big help in the music business, I can assure you.

"Every Jamaican artist knows that if I am their friend, no bad Americans, law enforcement or otherwise, will mess with them. While Bob is in New York, Paul and I will complete the deal to separate him from Island Records and that bambaclat Chris Blackwell. Bob will record for us going forward. We'll probably let him call it Tuff Gong so it will appear to the world it's his and he's broken free at last. We've already extricated him from that other thief, Don Taylor. Here's where you come in. You were smart to figure that this ska revival could happen in the US. I want the new label to be in on that from the get-go.

"I'm giving you a second and final chance. Bring Loraine into the label. I'll get artists to play your club. Or maybe you should come and work for us instead. Perhaps that's the way you convince her to sign willingly. If she still resists, you might want to tell her once I put it out there that I'm claiming her, no record company in the US will try to sign her. Ask around if you doubt that. Give it some thought. Go to Madison Square Garden tomorrow. We are playing before the Commodores to give Bob more exposure to a Black American audience. Come backstage and meet him afterward, and give me your decision as to which of those two options you prefer."

He handed James an envelope containing backstage passes.

James finished his drink. "Okay, Tony. I will but I'm not certain Loraine will listen to me no matter what I say."

"You know, I heard about the very near miss you both had outside your joint. Shame about Guy Harding. Perhaps it would be wise to avoid the possibility of not being so fortunate next time."

His message clearly delivered, Marshall saw James out.

He barely resisted the temptation to go back to Lauren Bacall's place to get her advice.

He got a cab and, by no means feeling ready to discuss this with Suzanne, had it take him to 213 Park Avenue South, which housed the club that had inspired him from afar in the glitter rock days of Bowie, Iggy Pop, and Lou Reed: Max's Kansas City. In recent years, after a brief closure, new club booker Peter Crowley had reinvented it as a punk venue, which made perfect sense to James given the undeniable links between the two genres.

He felt better just walking in under the—to him—hallowed awning. He wandered through the currently near-empty legendary back room before putting some coins in the jukebox and depositing himself upstairs at the bar. Initially as he drank, only one thing was crystal clear: Marshall had confidently shown his hand and in doing so had confirmed James's worst suspicions. But by the fourth Scotch and water, an idea came to him.

CHAPTER 35

AFTER PASSING OUT FOR eight hours, James woke the next afternoon feeling refreshed. He put the *Superfly* cassette on the stereo in his room. "Little Child Running Wild" instantly focused him on the moves he had to make.

He called the Miami number on the card Don Taylor had given him and after a five-minute hold Taylor's assistant connected them.

"Don, if I proved it was to your advantage, do you think you could quickly get your hands on the property leases Marshall signed in Jamaica?"

"Everything's gettable for me in Jamaica if I desire it, but why would I go to the trouble?"

"I don't have the time to negotiate, so I'll have to trust you. Marshall implied last night that the shooting of English singer Guy Harding outside my club was actually an attempt to shoot Loraine Sulley and probably me, which I already suspected.

"I need the leases to hold over his head to keep us alive. They will act as proof he's pocketed the mob's millions instead of outright buying those properties."

"I still don't see what's in it for me."

"Let's call it an exchange of information. If I tell you something to your benefit, will you get me the leases?"

"If you tell me first, before I have to go to the trouble of getting you the documents."

James knew the risk but time was too tight to do it any other way. "I know you hate him and presume you still see royalties from Island Records, so here's the deal. He's making a move while Bob Marley's in New York to seal a deal with him and Paul Castellano to get Marley out of the Island deal. They're starting a new label and he's hell-bent on getting Loraine to sign, too. The only way I see getting out of this is to have something on Marshall that will protect us. I figure if Castellano knew Marshall had ripped him off so badly, he'd off him, right?"

"That's what that rasclat's up to, is it? You know, you are a bit more cunning than I gave you credit for. As tempting as it is to say thank you and hang up, I'll get you the papers. I'm still curious about your singer, and you may just be worth more to me alive than dead.

"Just remember—this is not an even exchange as my life's not involved, so you will owe me another favor if I ever need it."

"Fair enough, Don. But it did cross my mind that if Bob Marley's contracts are still tied to you—management or otherwise—they might come for you, and clearly some kind of threat to Chris Blackwell will be involved to get him to roll over, right?"

"Yes, you're right. That's partly why my staying in the background while you threaten Marshall works for me, fortunately for you."

"How quickly can you get your hands on the documents? I'm supposed to go to the Madison Square Garden show tonight."

"Even I can't move that quickly. There's a second show at Madison Square Garden. You'll have to stall him a day. I'll have one of my boys in Kingston handle things in Jamaica. He can fly a set to you and, of course, make copies for me, as they will be useful for my own needs. Where are you staying? If I do this, I need you to find out as many details as possible on exactly how Marshall plans to get Bob out of his deal. It's imperative he isn't aware of my involvement so I have time to make the most out of the situation."

"Mate, that would be great. I'm at the Plaza. You are sure the estate agents there will hand them over?"

"You are joking, of course. Good luck and watch your back." As the *Superfly* title song played away, James felt strangely calm.

He called Marshall's number and left word that he had to come the next night instead, then tried Suzanne and was put right on with her.

"Sorry to mess around again, but can we go to Madison Square Garden on the twentieth instead?"

"I can make that work, James, but is everything okay? You sounded worried last night and you didn't show at Hurrah's or Danceteria."

"Yeah, I'm sorry. I needed some time to think after seeing Marshall. I know I keep stalling on this but I promise I'll fill you in at dinner. Did you get ahold of Loraine?"

"Yes, I did, but I'll fill you in when we have dinner." She mimicked his accent in a way that would have irritated him coming from anyone else but was teasingly fun from her.

"Alright, I suppose I deserve that."

"Yes, you do, but I forgive you. I might even have a surprise for you now, too."

"Oh, yeah? What might that be?"

"Let's stick to the Odeon idea. Don't be late now. Ta-ta."

He called Sylvia Robinson, who was coming into Manhattan again as it turned out, so they arranged to meet at Caffe Reggio.

Ed was on duty today and asked him how he was enjoying his visit.

"Well, it's hard to imagine that innocent Beatles time and all the girls outside, that's for sure."

"Yes, New York is a rather more dangerous place these days. But the Plaza is unchanged and I imagine that spirit will always abide here."

The cab took James down to MacDougal Street in Greenwich Village, where he could see Sylvia sitting at one of the four tables on the partly covered green patio outside, drinking coffee. The place, which proudly displayed the fact it had been around since 1929 and was the first place in America to serve cappuccino, had a different atmosphere than he'd imagined, but he was happy to see the bar and remember the inspirational moment from *Shaft* it rekindled.

He joined Sylvia and ordered a beer from the passing waiter. "So how did you feel about our meeting?" she asked.

"There's something about your records that feels like the future. I can't explain quite why, but I think it's going to feel right, mixed in with all the Jamaican-influenced music I already play."

"Funny you should say that. Now, I've been living in Jersey for the last fifteen years, but once I started catching up on what had been going on in the Bronx, a lot of people say this Jamaican kid DJ Kool Herc was the first, so maybe that's why."

"I didn't know that," he admitted. "Here's the thing, though. I really don't have the money to be flying a bunch of people to LA. As good as it would be to get rid of my law enforcement problems, not to mention some I have with Tony Marshall, I'm not sure that your partner Morris Levy is the right solution."

She put her hand over his and spoke to him in a tone reminiscent of her first hit, "Love Is Strange," back in the 1950s.

"When my husband Joe told me that he'd gone to Morris to solve our financial crisis and that he was now our partner, I could have killed him. I actually threatened to stop making the records, but he's promised me once we make some more hits that we will buy Levy out. That man is the devil, so you need to walk away now and don't ever go back to his office. If you are lucky, he will forget about you."

"What about the show, though? You agreed you need to do live shows on the West Coast, right?"

"None of these kids have booking agents yet, but yes, we do need to do it. Just not this way. Between Morris and if you have problems already with Tony Marshall, you'd best focus on getting out of New York alive."

"Thanks for the advice, and at least I'll have a good memory of finally getting to Caffe Reggio. I loved the scene here in *Shaft*."

"I guessed that's why you asked to meet here. Thing is, you ain't in no damn movie you saw back in London and personally, I have never met anyone remotely like John Shaft in this city."

CHAPTER 36

THE NEXT AFTERNOON, THE front desk called James in his room.

"There is a, uh, Mr. Jim Rockford downstairs with a package for you, but the gentleman insists on giving it to you personally. He says he's brought it from Jamaica and won't entrust it to our undoubted care."

"Alright. Send him up."

He opened the door and admitted a towering giant of a man dressed in a check jacket with beige pants and carrying a manila envelope.

"This has copies of the many leases that American boy Tony Marshall signed for on behalf of the Cayman Investment Group and paid for in cash for large estates around the coastline on the island."

James opened the envelope and started leafing through them. All the payments were in cash, so the idea must have been to launder the mob boss's ill-gotten gains. The signatures dated back almost a year and had renewal clauses written in. Marshall could never explain why he had leased instead of buying to Castellano. The fact that Marshall paid in cash meant he had millions of the mob boss's cash stashed that should have been used to purchase the land outright. If Castellano found out about this, Marshall was surely a dead man.

"Thank you so much. How did you manage to get all of them so quickly?"

"I solve people's problems in a hurry when necessary."

"Mate, I have to ask. Were you born with that name?"

"No, man. I love *The Rockford Files* TV show. I even have a tan '77 Firebird I drive 'round Kingston in. You live in Los Angeles, right? You ever been out to his place in Malibu?"

"No, but I love the show too. Tell you what—if you ever come to LA, I'll drive us out to Paradise Cove. We can go drink at that joint across from his trailer. Think it's called the Sandcastle."

James was glad he had guessed right. Not a huge leap given the Jamaican tradition of appropriating pop culture actor names as monikers.

"I'll take you up on that. My cousin has an Ital restaurant on Crenshaw called Jake's, and I've been meaning to get over and check it out. Listen. Don Taylor told me what this is all about. I'm going to stay at my sister's in the Bronx for a couple of nights. Call me if you need some backup, okay? A lot of us don't like how an American tried to talk Bob Marley out of making political music."

After Rockford left, James tried calling Denise Hamilton at the *LA Times* and as usual got her answering machine, but left a message detailing the latest. He then wrote letters to her and Detective Franc Mata before heading down to the front desk. He had them make three sets of Xerox copies of the lease agreements, putting one in each of the envelopes with the letters. He had the hotel send one each registered mail to Mata and Denise, and took one with him as he headed down to the Odeon in Tribeca on Thomas and West Broadway. The area was pretty desolate, with a dangerous edge until the cab got to the neon-lit sign that read "Odeon Cafeteria." The reddish-orange neon reminded him of old Odeon cinemas in the London of his childhood.

Inside, the warm lit room was clearly riffing on a French brasserie, but there was an almost LA noir feel that James instantly felt at home in. He was the first to arrive and was seated at a table next to the floor-to-ceiling window as Dinah Washington's "My Heart Cries for You" played on the sound system.

He'd just ordered a glass of Bordeaux when two hands reached out from behind him and covered his eyes. A moment's panic dissipated when Suzanne, who must now be in front of him, said, "Surprise."

The hands dropped to his shoulders and he turned his head, looking up into the sparkling green eyes of Loraine.

"Fuck me, girl. You gave me a scare but you are a sight for sore eyes."

Suzanne had apparently moved on from Chanel to a sharp black Dior suit tonight. He guessed Loraine had been shopping in London at Vivienne Westwood and Malcolm McLaren's Seditionaries, judging by the black leather bondage corset and skirt.

Despite the French tones, the woman who came over to take their order was cool, casual, and added to the sense that there was nothing stuffy about the place.

Suzanne ordered sole stuffed with salmon mousse, James liver with raisins in vinegar sauce, and Loraine burger and fries, the latter confirming this place didn't take itself too seriously.

"I like the choice, Suzanne. This place feels really different for New York."

"Yes, it's just opened but Warhol and Basquiat are already regulars, along with all the *Saturday Night Live* people. It's like that whole vile Studio 54 scene is finally over and everything's changing for the better, although walking Tribeca at night is still taking your life in your own hands."

The allusion to danger reminded James of the underlying reason he was here and the potentially deadly job immediately ahead. He was worried about Loraine being in New York while simultaneously hoping they would end up in bed together again.

"So, you two, I'm well surprised. What's the story? It's good to have you back, Loraine."

"You have Suzanne to thank for that. I didn't want to come, and I'm sure you know the reason why."

"I understand but I have a plan to make you safe from Marshall. Bob Marley's old manager Don Taylor showed up at the club the night

Top Ranking had originally been due to play. He hates Marshall and if he liked the show, had thought to manage you—partly to fuck with Marshall. He tells me that Marshall is ripping off Paul Castellano for millions in a Jamaican real estate deal. Better yet, he just got me proof I can hang over Marshall to make us safe from him."

The food arrived along with cocktails for Suzanne and Loraine, allowing James a short-lived moment of hope that this would put her mind at ease.

Loraine took a long sip. "Oh, James, being away from all this in England—where, although they can be very stuffy, at least no one shoots at each other—gave me perspective you have clearly lost. I'm on my way home. New York is just a layover and if Suzanne hadn't convinced me I should tell you in person, I wouldn't have even left JFK. Top Ranking are over. I called the band before I left London and told them."

"Loraine, when you gave me that tape and backed up your cocky attitude on stage, me and everyone in that room knew you had that indefinable thing that sets real artists apart from the rest. I know you won't entertain it, of course, but Marshall's pulling a move to get Marley out of Island and wanted you to be the other artist he starts a new label with. He may be a gangster but he knows you can be big. Once we remove his threat, there'll be other, more legitimate people who'll want to do the same. Don't throw it away. That would be letting him win."

"He could be right, you know. You might always wonder what might have been," said Suzanne.

"I've made up my mind. Besides, I was only able to get a three-week visa this time, and if Reagan becomes president, it's only going to get harder for people like me. Duncan and I might try writing some songs together. After losing Guy, Vortex have already decided they won't even consider looking for a new singer. They were band as gang, James, the way you believe in. Duncan and I can maybe help each other move past all this. We can disappear in Jamaica as long as I stay away from Kingston."

"Are you two..." said James, instantly regretting it.

Loraine looked at him sadly and shook her head as "Remember Walking in the Sand" by the Shangri-Las played.

The three of them barely went back to their food and once the drinks were finished, Suzanne handed her AmEx corporate card to a passing waiter.

"There's two cars waiting outside, one to take Loraine to JFK and the other will whisk us up to Madison Square Garden," said Suzanne.

Outside, Loraine put her arms around him tight and kissed him hard. "Don't lose yourself here, James. I can see you are in danger of that. You are a true punk at heart, and you may think you are tough enough but you aren't a killer and people like Marshall are. I saw that in Kingston as well, with people like him. I hope one day you'll understand why things with us weren't meant to be right now."

CHAPTER 37

As THE CAR TOOK them up toward Midtown, Suzanne said, "Do you still need to put yourself through confronting Marshall now that you know Loraine doesn't want to be here anyway and the band's over?"

"Yeah. I'm starting to realize there's a lot of these kind of guys around and if I start backing down now, I may never stop."

"Don't let that be what I have to put on your tombstone. I couldn't handle another funeral so soon."

"I'm betting on Marshall not doing anything at Madison Square Garden. And once he knows I could bury him by giving those leases to Castellano, it should end his threat. He may be tougher than tough but no one rips off the mob and lives. Those leases are essentially a death certificate."

"What about you and Loraine? Had you fallen for her?"

"Nah, not really. She's cool and I love her voice and attitude, but we never spent that much time together," said James, trying to convince himself as much as Suzanne.

"For whatever it's worth, I'm guessing she and Duncan aren't lovers, at least not yet. I doubt that she and Guy would have lasted but no one can quite compete with a beautiful ghost of a memory."

"Yeah, I know what you mean." James thought of his one night with Sue Ann. *Why did his most vivid memory always have to be her walking up the steps of the plane?*

"Did you and Guy have a thing? I wondered as he was flirting with you when we first met."

"He was adorable and a lovely guy but I wouldn't dream of sleeping with any artist on the label. Women have a hard enough time getting taken seriously without proving half the guys at labels who say that we are glorified groupies right. Anyway, most singers are narcissistic by nature and I want someone who likes me more than the mirror."

"Good point. Are you seeing anyone?"

"Well, I'm not beyond taking a cute boy home for the night, but that's all I want or need right now. My friends in the downtown scene wouldn't think twice about heading out for the night with one guy and going home with a different one. There's so many to choose from and sleeping with friends is so easy. No one expects it to be more than that night. The boys don't mind and more than a few of the band guys are quite fond of sleeping with each other too."

The car eased its way up Madison to the circular Madison Square Garden, which was primarily used for basketball and hockey games but plenty of bands like the Stones, Led Zeppelin, and the Who had played multiple shows at the 20,000-seat venue since it opened in 1968.

"Bob Marley's been doing loads of interviews ahead of this, and I'm curious how the crowd who are here for the Commodores will react. I expect you know his US audiences up to now have been nearly all white kids and it's clear he's making an attempt to change that," said Suzanne.

Waving their passes at the security guys at one of the multiple entrances was enough to easily access them, although Suzanne refused to stick it to her Dior jacket, eventually compromising by attaching it to her tiny purse.

Kurtis Blow was onstage, rapping away, as they made their way down the sharply banked rows of seats. But much of the crowd seemed bemused, although the many Jamaicans who were way more familiar with the idea of a DJ and toaster combo seemed appreciative of his set, which ended shortly after they sat. As Bob Marley and the

Wailers walked onstage in red, gold, and green satin bomber jackets and jeans, James surveyed the audience's dress.

Outside of the Jamaicans, who were mostly favoring the same Rastafarian colors as the band, the rest was like a trip through the seventies, from the *Superfly* styles he loved to the dayglow disco he despised.

He was shocked at how gaunt Marley looked compared to the show he'd seen at the Lyceum in London five years ago. But he and the band sounded as fierce and inspiring as ever.

There was a moment between songs, though, where James thought the singer was going to collapse as he appeared to steady himself on an amp. After just under an hour, the defiant and politically charged set had the entire crowd on their feet, exiting after "Could You Be Loved."

"So great, huh, James?"

"Yeah, and if I had any lingering doubts that maybe I shouldn't go through with this confrontation with Marshall, I don't now. How could anyone run away after the messages of that set?"

"I'll come with you."

"No. There's no point in him wondering if you are involved. Just point me to where the backstage entrance is. If I'm not back by the time the Commodores finish, here's Jim Rockford's number at his sister's. Call him, okay?"

He got through the first layer of security and was admitted to the stone-walled area he could see led to team dressing rooms. The Commodores, all in white suits, were exiting the home-team one, clearly about to go onstage. But as he continued, he was halted by three more MSG security men. James pointed to his pass.

"No one's going back there, you included, pal, so blow."

James spotted Marshall's man from the Dakota coming out of the away team dressing room. "Oi, oi, Alfio. I'm supposed to be seeing your boss."

The man glared at him but went back inside and returned after a couple of minutes, pushing through the three-man wall that separated them. He came way closer to James than he needed to speak over the muted sound of the Commodores' "Easy."

"Mr. Marshall is too busy to see you. Be at the Dakota at noon before we leave for Pittsburgh. Don't be late. You never know. Your life may depend on it."

The thin smile was the first change of expression James had seen the man make, along with the first sentences he'd spoken.

He made the trek back, stepping into the sound of "Brick House," along with an explosion of lights and pyrotechnics that stood in stark contrast to the Wailers' lighting that employed almost as few as the meager ones at the O.N. Klub.

He sat down next to Suzanne.

"That was quick. Everything okay?"

"No. I don't get it but he wouldn't see me. His boy said I'm to be at the Dakota at noon."

"James, I don't like the sound of that." She took his hand. "You shouldn't go. Maybe he got wind of what you've been up to. I mean, if your friend Jim Rockford strong-armed the real estate guys, maybe they called Marshall?"

"I hadn't thought of that but the real estate guys wouldn't know about me. Shit…unless someone who knows Rockford saw him at the Plaza. Could Marshall have someone keeping an eye on my comings and goings? I don't see it, though. We are just getting paranoid."

"James. He's a killer. It's not being paranoid but going could be construed as suicidal."

"Can we go and call Jim Rockford? I have an idea."

"Of course. You can call from my place. I think you should stay the night. In most respects, you'll be safer there." She grinned.

They exited the Garden as "Three Times a Lady" put the final nail in the coffin of a band he'd loved when he first heard "Machine Gun" back at the Speakeasy in '74 but now sounded cheesy as hell, especially after the riveting authentic power of the Wailers.

CHAPTER 38

IT HAD TURNED COOLER and there was a bite to the autumn air as James and Jim stood waiting for the elevator at the Dakota. James was glad he'd worn his long black Granny Takes a Trip coat with velvet collar he'd bought from the beyond cool rock and roll tailors on the Kings Road in London but rarely got opportunities to use in LA.

"Hopefully she's willing to help, but if not, we'll have to take a more direct approach," said James.

"No problem, man. I'm ready for anything."

James pressed the buzzer and a few seconds later, the door opened.

"Well, look who's back…and with a friend. Would you boys like to come in?" she drawled in that signature voice that made James feel like he'd stepped into a noir dream.

"Thanks, Ms. Bacall. This is Jim Rockford."

"Well, you sure look different, Jim," she said.

"Waittaminute. I saw you in that two-episode story of *The Rockford Files* last year. 'Lions, Tigers, Monkeys and Dogs.' You were wicked in that, lady," said Jim.

"You said things were a little dull, so I was hoping you might be willing to help us," said James.

"True. And they have asked me to come back for another episode, so keeping in practice with Jim Rockford here might not be a bad idea. What's the story?"

"Marshall poses a threat to the life of a singer friend of mine from Jamaica, and me, for that matter. He pretty much admitted last time I was here that he'd arranged a previous hit attempt on us that resulted in the death of English singer Guy Harding outside my club in LA."

"Hmm. He goes that far, does he? Are you sure?"

"I know you think he's a nightclub owner. I think he's a drug dealer, a killer by remote control, and a suborner of crooked cops. He's whatever looks good to him."

Giving James her most laconic look, she said, "Well, you certainly know your lines from *The Big Sleep*. The question is, can you live out the solution in real life, kiddo?"

"I have something to hold over Marshall now to protect us, thanks to Jim here. I'm going to confront him, but we need to put his boy Alfio on ice in your place while I do it."

She gave this a moment's thought before nodding.

James and Jim stood on either side of Marshall's door while Bacall rang the buzzer. After a moment, Alfio opened the door. "What's up, lady?"

Rockford stepped in, putting a Magnum .45 against the side of Alfio's head and James followed suit, pressing a finger to his lips for silence. He dug into Alfio's suit jacket, removing his weaponry before Rockford ushered the mobster to the next-door apartment.

James walked solo down the long corridor, retracing his steps from last time, glancing at rooms along the way to make sure there were no other visitors. He entered the library, quietly closing the door behind him in the hope Marshall wouldn't notice Alfio's absence. He was rewarded by the sight of an absorbed Marshall lounging on the same sofa, reading the *New York Times*, dressed in a brown jogging suit.

"I couldn't see you last night because Bob was feeling unwell and wanted privacy. He called from the Essex House this morning, though, feeling much improved, and said he was going to go jogging in Central Park. We may see him run by. I'll join him after our business is concluded."

He stood, turning to look out at the panoramic view of Central Park. "So did you decide to come and work for me, or will it just be me handling young Loraine's career as Bob's label mate? Perhaps you, too, will have a beautiful view and a new home soon if things go well.

"None of the above."

"You know, it's funny but Alfio took an instant dislike to you. He mumbled something about some limey rock and roller defiling his sister, and I fear you look a bit like the man. I think Stevie Marriott was his name. Anyway, I think I'll have him hang you upside down out of this window. I understand that method is often effectively employed by English record man Don Arden when boys like you get out of line. The thing is, I may just want to terrify you into acquiescence. But Alfio, I fear, may not be able to resist letting go. I implore you to change your mind before I call him in."

James walked and stood next to him. "First off, Alfio was called away unexpectedly, so he won't be doing any dangling. Secondly, you might want to really make the most of this view 'cause if you don't do what I tell you to, it could all crumble around you very quickly."

He pulled the folded manila envelope out of his inside coat pocket and flattened it hard against Marshall's chest.

"I imagine if one of the copies of these, which I put in certain people's hands, was delivered to Mr. Castellano, he'd do a lot worse than dangle you out a fucking window."

Marshall removed the sheaf of leases and started leafing through them.

"I expect you stashed the millions in cash he gave you to buy all those properties in the Caymans. Not that that's much help if you've got a couple of bullets in the back of your head and you're dead in a New Jersey ditch or some other shithole. I have a feeling that this kind of betrayal might result in a nice bit of excruciating torture first, though. What do you think, Tony? Maybe you'd be pissing yourself like you made Loraine do at the Beverly Hills Hotel, you fucking cunt."

Marshall, clearly seething, managed to keep control. "What do you want for all the copies?"

"If anything untoward ever happens to me, Loraine, or any of our friends, now or in the future, a set go to your boy."

"Hmm. Perhaps you are learning how to survive in this business, Englishman. Anything else?"

The phone rang. Marshall walked over and answered.

"Are you certain?...How can they be sure?...How long does he have?...Tell no one, you understand? Yes. Including Rita. I said no one. We'll go to Pittsburgh for the next show. I need time to plan."

He hung up, closing his eyes for a long moment, clearly composing himself. "Well, you have gone to a lot of trouble for next to nothing. I no longer have an urgent need for your girl. There will be no record label. Bob Marley collapsed in the park. That was his friend Skill Cole calling from the hospital. They say Bob only has a month to live. If there's nothing else you want, you should leave. I have things to attend to."

"That's horrible news, Tony. But listen, there's one other thing. A bit of advice. I'd suggest you cut your ties with Detective Johnny Holton. That boy's gone off the deep end—capping those dealers in LA, in case you didn't know. A straight-arrow LAPD cop's onto him, so I'd cover your tracks if I were you."

"So that little bitch did hear things she shouldn't have. Why are you telling me this?"

"For whatever it's worth, she didn't know shit. I only realized it was Holton you were in the smack business with after Guy Harding was killed. So the shooting outside my club is what started all your shit unraveling. I need Holton permanently out of my hair, too, and now it's in your best interests to be rid of him as well before they nail him. If he talks, they'll trace everything back to you and Castellano. I'll leave it up to you to figure that out."

James turned and walked back down the long corridor.

Marshall called out. "Now you are requesting murder for your own convenience, Englishman. Perhaps you are more like me than you think."

CHAPTER 39

LAUREN BACALL ADMITTED JAMES into her opulent Louis XIII-inspired mansion-sized apartment.

He followed her and the cocker spaniel along a pale-blue and wood hallway past an array of rooms, all of which were stuffed with antique furniture, collectable art, and high-end bric-a-brac. Her open-necked men's style white cotton shirt, tight black pants, and elegant boots accentuated her stunning frame.

"Wow, Ms. Bacall, this is almost like having a mansion inside a building."

"It is quite a size, isn't it? And larger than even John Lennon and Yoko Ono's place on the seventh floor."

They entered the rusty-red and deep-blue dining room to find Rockford drinking a small bottle of imported Kronenbourg beer, while using a trussed Alfio as a footstool.

"Mission accomplished, James?"

"Yeah, this part, at least, thanks to you two. Although there's still the issue of the crooked cops back in LA to deal with."

"What shall we do with laughing boy here?" Rockford gave the prone gangster a sharp kick in the ribs, which elicited a string of expletives.

"Good question. I hear our boy hates English guys because one of us deflowered his sister. Apparently, the plan, if I didn't deliver

Loraine, was to have Alfio hang me out the window but Marshall feared that this guy might not be able to resist dropping me. That true, Alfio?"

"You fucking limey rock and rollers are all the same. I'll kill you and that little prick Stevie Marriott if I ever see either of you again."

Rockford rose this time and gave the guy a much harder kick. "Language, Alfio. There's a lady present. I think if Ms. Bacall doesn't object, the best solution is to let me throw him off the balcony. The cops will quickly link him back to Marshall."

Alfio hurled a string of curses at the Jamaican, who took the fine linen towel from the dining table and stuffed it down the Italian's throat, ending his part in the conversation.

"Look, boys, I can happily play the noir role that you and most people erroneously presume to be my personality all day, but if it's all the same to you, perhaps returning him where you found him might be simpler in the long run. My home is not a film set."

"She's right, Jim. And besides, Marshall may well do that job for us as Alfio didn't exactly fulfill his function when we came knocking. Ms. Bacall, if you wouldn't mind letting me use your phone, I think it's time we thanked you and got out of your hair."

She led him to her study and as he sat to call Suzanne, the cocker spaniel leapt onto his lap and, putting front paws on his shoulder, leaned her head against his cheek.

"That speaks well for you, James, as she doesn't like most men. I'd suggest that if you make it through all this that you strongly consider getting a dog. You'll never go wrong with a spaniel. They'll always keep you on the right track."

Suzanne insisted on picking them up so she could get the full story.

Rockford slung Alfio over his shoulder, looking wistfully at the balcony he would love to have tossed the man off of, and the three of them followed the actress back to her front door.

"Well, it's been fun, gentleman. I hope your noir story ends well, James."

"Thank you for the help and inspiration when I really needed it. The noirs you were in ended well enough so that's what I'm aiming for."

Rockford threw Alfio against Marshall's door. He landed in a tangle after a satisfying thud, and they took the elevator down to the street, where Suzanne was waiting in a black stretch limo.

"Since you have survived this far, it's best to get you out of New York while the getting's good. I suggest we get you checked out of the Plaza and straight to JFK. I had my office put you on the next flight back to LA, okay?"

"Suzanne, you've been above and beyond great but this must have all cost a fortune."

"Don't be silly. When I got this job, they gave me a six-figure expense account and said to make sure it was all used, otherwise it would get trimmed the following year. I don't even have to fill in receipts. My assistant sends the monthly American Express bill to accounting and they simply pay it."

"Now that's my kind of job. Where do I apply?" said Rockford.

James ran into the Plaza while Suzanne and Jim waited and grabbed his bag from the room before checking out and, of course, his room and incidentals had also been covered by the trusty label AmEx.

"So long, James. You're leaving in a limo just like the Beatles did. You English kids seem to do alright here, huh?" Ed, the doorman, opened the stretch's door with a flourish.

James sank back into the seat next to Suzanne, suddenly weary as some of the tension of the last few days dropped away in the cocooned air-conditioned comfort.

"You ready to go home, too, Jim?" James asked, looking across to the facing bench seat.

"I'm going to stick around one more night. I don't get to see my sister very often."

"Mate, I can't thank you enough. I'd probably be dead right now if not for all you've done, but I have to tell you some very bad news I got from Marshall. He got a call while I was there saying Bob Marley was just told he only has a month to live."

Suzanne gasped. "How can that be?"

"I don't know any details. I thought he looked really gaunt at the show last night but figured they've been on the road so long that he was just exhausted. Apparently he wasn't feeling well after the show but went jogging this morning and collapsed in Central Park. For whatever reason, Marshall's keeping it a secret from everyone too, including Rita Marley."

"That is a tragedy for Jamaica. After the assassination attempt, it felt like he was immortal. I'll call Don Taylor from my sister's. He'll know what to do."

They traversed the wilds of the Bronx, the limo an incongruous sight in the crime-ridden neighborhood, and Jim climbed out in front of a tenement building.

"Look after yourself, Jim. I hope we get to Malibu one day, mate."

"You need to come to Kingston and see where all this music you play comes from, man."

James and Suzanne were silent for a while.

But as they neared JFK, he said, "Will you let Loraine know she's safe now?"

"I can't, James. She wouldn't give me any details as to where exactly she was going. She felt it was safer that way. Are you going to carry a torch for her? I thought you might manage not to if last night was any indication." She pressed her finger hard into the palm of his hand teasingly.

The car swept up to the Pan Am entrance and halted. "You're something else, Suzanne." He grinned.

CHAPTER 40

THE PLANE CIRCLED ABOVE the vast expanse of Los Angeles that overwhelmed many visitors but felt its usual welcoming self to James. He was listening to the Clash's first record, which had helped galvanize him to finally get out and do something with his life in the first place.

"White Riot" and the rest pulsed through every part of him, their angry energy leaving him ready to do whatever it took to keep the club going.

He was only half surprised to see a peak-capped and uniformed livery woman holding a sign with his name on it as he walked past baggage claim.

"My name's Alison. I'm yours for the night, courtesy of Suzanne Black."

Once ensconced in the back, he used the bulky phone in the central console to call Detective Franc Mata, who happened to answer the line himself.

"I just landed, Franc, and figured you'd want an update."

"So you made it out in one piece. I'm surprised, especially when I got your envelope. That was a crazy stunt to try."

"Listen, you gave me a beginner's education into regional Mexican cuisine, how about I do the same for you with English food and football?"

"I don't have time to go to Santa Monica to one of those pubs."

"Nah, I hate those places and that whole whining ex-pat thing about how they miss proper English this that and the other. They should all just fuck off back there as far as I'm concerned. I'm talking about the Cock 'n Bull up on the west end of the Strip. It's been there since the 1930s and is more like an old Hollywood fantasy of an English joint. Much better than the real thing. On top of that, PBS has deemed English football culturally relevant and they show one tape-delayed match a week. It's the Manchester derby and my team United are home to City today. I have to see it."

"Alright, you convinced me. See you in an hour," the bemused cop said, wondering why football seemingly was as important as discussing saving his own neck to this kid.

The driver smoothly detoured west a few blocks as there was an accident on Doheny.

She turned right onto Sunset in the midst of the mansions and manicured lawns of Beverly Hills. Even though the early evening air was still hot, James could swear it dropped ten degrees here as the hissing water sprayers shot over every manicured lawn. He loved how each home was completely different, especially the 1930s and '40s built ones. He was shaken out of this reverie as they passed a more gaudy mansion when he saw that the white statues lining the front of its lawn had had crudely drawn penises added.

"What the fuck."

The driver caught the direction of his gaze in her rearview mirror. "Yeah. That's the Shah of Iran's place. I hear he or his wife did the new artwork."

"I bet the neighbors love that."

"I grew up on Elm Drive. They don't like change around here and a bunch of oil-rich immigrants moving in is not going down well. My grandparents are beside themselves. They escaped Europe during World War Two and believe you should quietly assimilate."

"And what do you think?"

"I couldn't care less who moves in, but I don't like these cheesy Greco-Roman villas, complete with dopy pillars replacing the Spanish Colonial or faux country estate homes we all played in as kids."

"Yeah, I'm with you there."

She pulled over at 9170 Sunset Boulevard right in front of the striped awning. A large light pole was attached to the roof, topped by a gas lamp. Below, in Olde English script, *The Cock 'n Bull*, lit the discreet neon sign.

"I love this place. My parents bought me here as a kid. I've seen Bette Davis, Peter O'Toole, Orson Welles—all kinds of people. Take your time. I'll be waiting."

"If I wasn't meeting a cop, I'd invite you in. Listen, I don't live far from here. I'll get a cab later."

"Too bad. Suzanne's office told me to be prepared for a late night." She scrawled a 275 number on the back of her business card. "Call me sometime. I'll take you on a tour of the coolest old homes."

James grabbed his bag, bounced through the heat into the cool of the old tavern, and grabbed a seat at the bar just underneath the small TV screen that hung discreetly above the old wooden façade. He glanced along the bar at the row of elegantly dressed old guys sipping martinis or Moscow mules served in copper mugs. Many, he knew from previous conversations, were screenwriters from the forties who'd done well, built now-paid-off Beverly Hills homes, and were happily coasting on shared memories. Only a few miles east but a world away were joints like the Frolic Room or the Firefly, where guys whose dice had fallen the other way told tales of misfortune and near misses. He ordered a Pimm's as he watched the two mutually hated rival teams walk out onto the pitch at his beloved Old Trafford in Manchester, barely noticing as Detective Mata slid onto the stool next to him.

"Good timing, Franc. Let me order you one of these. It's like a summer drink in England and apart from not being able to get quite the right lemonade in the States, this place makes it pretty well."

Mata acquiesced but looked a bit askance at the cucumber and fruit that floated on the top when the formally dressed bartender returned with his.

"Yeah. It's a bit 'froufrou,' especially for watching a match. None of this crowd would approve," James admitted, looking up at the seething mass of standing, chanting United fans in the Stretford End on the screen.

"Jesus Christ. It looks insane there. I can't make out what they are chanting," said the detective.

"Mostly semi-obscene, joyful, hate-filled lyrics to the tune of old songs. Trust me, on derby day, Manchester is like a ghost town. The shop owners board up the windows and close down. No one goes out for fear of running into marauding supporters. Other than the fact they don't have guns there, going to matches prepared me quite well for living here, mate."

"Speaking of which, I want the whole story of how you got out of New York alive. I was pretty sure I was going to be rid of you."

"I love you, too, Detective. Will you let me order for us? We can get an appetizer here and dinner is served buffet style through there." James pointed to the wood-paneled dining room across the way, which, with its real fireplace and wooden tables, resembled an English cottage. He asked for two Welsh Rabbits before starting in.

"You obviously got my note and the leases."

"Yeah, but first off, those transactions took place in Jamaica and aren't illegal, even though you are probably right and it was likely done with cash that Castellano wanted laundered."

"I get it, Franc. I'll give you what I got and you can decide what, if anything, you can do with it. I went to save me and Loraine and if I'd listened to you and gone in with a wire, I'd be dead. Marshall is paranoid enough to have checked me for that before he said a thing, okay?"

The cop grunted a begrudging acknowledgment.

"So he basically admitted to having the hit put on Loraine and me that resulted in Guy's death because he thought she heard more of him and Holton's conversation than she did. Throw in that he doesn't take no as an acceptable answer from women, and it was all the motivation he needed."

The bartender slid two small side plates containing melted cheese sauce on crispy toast across the bar. James kept one eye on the so far goalless match above while he watched Mata cut off a piece and try the dripping concoction.

"Hmm, not bad but there's no rabbit in this."

"Yeah, I've never known why it's called that. They certainly weren't averse to eating rabbits in England when I was a kid. Anyway, after I mailed the package to you, I went to confront Marshall at the Marley show, where I thought he wouldn't try anything, but he blew me off.

"I finally saw him at his opulent home at the Dakota. I won't go into details as I imagine some of this shit wasn't strictly by your book but I'm able to see him alone and drop the leases on him. I tell him that if anything untoward happens to me, Loraine, or anyone close to me that Castellano will be sent the evidence that he's been ripped off for a few mill and made to look a fool. Then he gets a call saying Bob Marley's been taken to hospital and only has a month to live, which obviously ends the planned label hustle with Castellano, too, so, all in all, a tough day for our Tony boy."

The restaurant door opened and a dozen or so sweaty men in football shorts led by Rod Stewart poured noisily into the bar behind them (no doubt returning from their weekly match, up by the Beverly Hills fire station) just as Steve Coppell scored for United on the screen above.

"How about we grab our dinners and you can give me your latest?" said James.

They took large white plates from the silver buffet table and surveyed the variety of roasted meats and vegetables.

"Alright, Franc, I know the English cliché is roast beef, and go for it if you must, but I'd say the pork with crackling would be the better bet. Either way, you have to try these." He spooned a round, perfectly cooked puffy Yorkshire pudding onto his plate. He added five of the roasted potatoes, eschewing the slightly less appealing green vegetables on display.

The detective largely followed James's suit, although added a slice of beef to his pork.

There was a loud groan from Rod Stewart as they reclaimed their barstools, City having just equalized.

Mata took an appreciative first bite of the pork and the crispy fat that topped it. "You know, this is pretty good and maybe the first thing in common I can see between our cultures."

"Detective, give me your news, and I hope it's as good as the pork."

"I visited Francisco with some graphic photographs of his friends dead in their hospital beds with throats slit. I told him that happened while they were under police guard and wondered if he had any theories about how such a terrible thing could have happened. I explained how I would like to avoid a similar fate befalling him."

James smiled, picturing the asshole between a rock and a hard place. "I like your style, Detective. Did he give up Holton?"

"Not exactly, but he was scared enough to agree to make a full statement and testify if we put him in witness protection. I said I needed something before starting the process. Also that we can put him and the Ford Custom outside your joint that night, so he's facing a murder rap too. He started to crumble a bit—fortunately, as the ballistics on his gun don't match the bullets that killed your friend. He wouldn't cop to the murder but admitted that he was dealing for a cop and pleaded for me to put him somewhere safe. I dropped a picture of Holton in front of him. He was terrified but looked away without speaking.

"I got him put in solitary while I process paperwork through the district attorney's office. It's going to take a while but if he fingers Holton, Internal Affairs will get on it. Best watch your back in the meantime. You may think you're safe now, but who knows if Holton will care what's good for Marshall?"

James felt an amphetamine-like rush at the thought of nailing Holton as a marauding United tore through City and defender Arthur

Albiston scored his first ever goal. James ordered more drinks and they both watched as United pressed for a third goal. But with a minute to go and totally against the run of play, City scored an equalizer, killing his mood. The BBC commentator said the draw might make the streets of Manchester safe tonight.

James doubted that just as much as whether the streets of LA were safe for him yet.

CHAPTER 41

JAMES SPENT THE NEXT month or so utterly focused on keeping the club buzzing and did his best to put the potential menace of Holton out of his mind. He called Rockford and got an introduction to his cousin Jake. James had a great meal at Jake's little joint on Crenshaw, of crispy fried whole trout and fried bammy, along with many Red Stripe beers. The trout was so perfectly fried he ate the bones too. By the end of the night, he and Jake had figured out a plan to have Jake set up a small food stand at the side of the club's dressing room and sell easy-to-eat dishes like ackee and saltfish and jerk pork. Jake would keep all the money and James would keep Mata and the Rampart cops out of his hair—hopefully.

Chrysalis man Michael Goldstone along with ace *BAM* magazine writer Mitch Schneider made his year by bringing the Specials down to hang out at the club.

James's best memory from the hazy night was when they told him that his turntables were pitched so fast it made their album sound like a live show when they were particularly wired.

Denise Hamilton was building her *LA Times* story but had reluctantly agreed to hold back on running anything related to the arrest of Francisco or his dead partners, and, in return, Mata had agreed to give her an exclusive tip-off before any official statements were made.

James rolled out of bed the first Saturday in December, finally giving in to the incessantly ringing phone. "Yeah. What do you want?"

"Is that any way to answer your phone? Thought you might like to know we got Francisco's testimony. Internal Affairs and the DA's office have okayed Holton's arrest. As far as we can tell his partner's clean, although I find it hard to believe," said Mata.

"Nice one, Detective. Come down to the club tonight, and I'll buy you a beer."

"If I ever come down there again, it'll be to close you down, kid. Keep your nose clean and make sure food's there every night, not just occasionally."

James wondered how the cop knew Jake's "soon come" Jamaican spirit had meant occasional no-shows. Surely he didn't have someone inside, watching every weekend?

The door buzzer sounded as James hung up. A twinge of fear. *Had Holton got word somehow?* He opened the door and took the package from England that his mailman said required a signature. Back upstairs, he cut through the brown cardboard wrapper to reveal several unmarked white label vinyl records. Inside was a hand-scrawled note from the Clash manager, publicist, and MC, Kosmo Vinyl. "Joe's happy you got your club going, and we like what we've heard about it from Sue Sawyer at Epic Records. Thought you might like an advance copy of *Sandinista* to play there."

Christmas got here early, huh? He instantly knew his DJ set before the Boxboys show tonight would be built around the Clash. He called Drea, Norman, Denise, and Patrick, telling them they had to come down to hear it and then spent the afternoon immersed in the sprawling three-album manifesto. As soon as he heard "The Magnificent Seven," he could tell the Clash were feeling the New York hip-hop scene too.

❂❂❂

THE BLACK BOMBER HE'D dropped was beginning to kick in as he got out of Lenny's cab.

Boxboys drummer Greg, dressed in his latest Clash-inspired clothing iteration, was leaning in the ticket window, talking to Louise. James carried his milk crate of records back around the bar and down to the turntables next to where she sat.

"James. Alberto's not shown up, which is really strange. He's always here, huh? I hope he's okay. Anyway, Greg said he'd work the door until their set time."

"Really? Thanks, mate. Really good of you. We can pay you in beers, okay? You gotta check IDs, though, alright? Plus, you ain't gonna believe this but I just got an advance of the Clash triple album. You lot better be good tonight 'cause you'll be following a heavy dose of it."

"No problem. We're always good and the Clash'll just rev me up more."

James eased into *Sandinista* with "One More Time" and "The Call Up" while the room gradually filled.

Norman must have picked Drea up as they arrived together. The Belfast man commandeered a couple of stools at the bar and yelled across at James. "Hey, man, this stuff sounds a bit melancholy. Can you crank it up a bit? Play me some Otis Redding."

Even though James realized he was right, he yelled back, "You know I don't take requests, squire."

The serious ska kids who were now filling the floor near the stage admittedly were struggling, though, so he got on the mike.

"Oi, oi. Dedicating this set to all the crooked cops in LA, especially the ones who thought tear gassing you lot was the way to go."

The Clash's "Guns of Brixton," "Police & Thieves," "I Fought the Law," and Jimmy Cliff's "The Harder They Come" followed in quick succession. He dropped the white label *Sandinista* advance to "Police on My Back" and flipped the strobe light, which had the desired effect of causing total frenzy in the crowd.

He heard a yell from Greg at the door and then half saw him bounce off the cashier's window. Louise screamed, leaping from her stool as two yellow snakeskin cowboy boots vaulted through the open window, followed by the rest of Detective John Holton. The staccato effect of the strobe gave a surreal look to everything and disoriented the cop, buying James a split second to flip the mike switch open and segue into the Clash's "Somebody Got Murdered."

Holton pulled a Colt M1911 out from his matching yellow snakeskin belt. "I've been sold out. I hear they're coming for me in the morning, so if I'm finished in this town, you're going to be too. You talk a big noir game, and I'm giving you the perfect ending to one. You and I are heading for the border tonight but you won't be coming all the way. Let's go, Dual, or do you want me to give it to you here? Either way, you die tonight." His voice boomed across the club.

"You're the killer cop, Detective Holton. You've just announced it to everyone in this joint. What do you think the best plan is?"

"Move it or you won't be the only one dying tonight."

He jammed the gun against James's ribs, who, amphetamine bravery aside, realized he needed to buy time and started walking down behind the bar. The crowd was frozen now but the lights still flickered eerily across the room. Bodies parted as Holton nudged James toward the door.

As they approached the end of the bar exit, a beefy hand shoved James sideways and Norman's other hand swung and smashed his bottle of beer in Holton's face. The cop dropped the gun as his hands went to his face, desperately pulling shards of glass out, screaming in agony and rage. James crawled across the floor and grabbed the gun.

Holton, blood pouring down his face from the cuts and his shattered nose, stared down at James. "Go on then, killer. Now's your one chance. Better take it if you've got the guts."

James rose to his knees and leveled the heavy gun, hearing the "dead forever" lyric ring mournfully across the room. He felt rage for Guy's snuffed-out life and started to squeeze the trigger.

"James, don't. It's over. You don't have to do this." Drea squatted down next to him. James didn't react but didn't pull the trigger any further.

"He's a fucking cop. In this town, they'll fix things up and charge you with murder," said Drea.

Holton sneered. He wiped the blood dripping in his eyes from the deep gash cut into his forehead. He then doubled over toward James; it appeared the cop was about to pass out. But Holton slid his right hand into a snakeskin boot, then straightened up, raising the revolver he kept there for backup.

Two booming gunshots rang out simultaneously, with someone saying, "Drop it."

This time Holton did fall all the way down, with two gaping holes in his back.

His partner, Fred Ostrow, stepped all the way into the club, service revolver pointed toward James. "Your life's in the balance here, limey. Give me just the slightest excuse."

James carefully lowered his arm and laid Holton's Colt on the floor.

Drea kicked it toward the advancing cop. "Don't even think about it. There's hundreds of people watching."

Ostrow stepped forward, picked the gun up by the barrel, and dropped it in his gray suit jacket pocket.

Sirens were ringing outside and several uniformed cops entered, along with Mata, who, surveying the scene, yelled, "Someone turn the damn strobe lights off!"

CHAPTER 42

LOUISE, REMARKABLY CALM, HAD not only turned the house lights on but figured putting on the Specials' "You're Wondering Now" might help keep things calm. The cops were slowly letting the crowd out after gathering statements from those close enough to provide coherent accounts of what they had witnessed.

Meanwhile, a less calm Mata quizzed Detective Fred Ostrow while James, Drea, Norman, Denise, and Patrick observed just within earshot at the bar.

"I gave you a heads up we were coming for your partner in the morning so we could do it smoothly and safely. How the fuck did this go down?"

"I figured it best to keep an eye on him tonight so I followed him when our shift ended. When he headed in here, I knew it might get ugly, so I parked. When I got in and saw Johnny about to off the kid, I felt I had to do something."

"So you shoot your own partner in the back to protect some punk kid you had just as big a hard-on for. C'mon now, Detective. You can do better than that."

Ostrow gave a good show of bristling, his straight-arrow, self-righteous-cop-from-the-1950s demeanor fully intact. "That's what you do to a mad dog, Detective Mata. Even if that dog was your best friend. Once it's mad, you shoot it, in my book."

"We needed Holton alive. He was the only link to where the smack was coming from. The only one who could have testified against the next guy up the chain. You haven't heard the end of this."

Ostrow straightened his hat, turned on his heel, and headed out, pushing past the exiting punters.

Mata walked to the barstools James and the others sat on, drinking much-needed beers. "I'm going to need your full statement, Dual, but while it's fresh in your mind...did Detective Ostrow make any attempt to stop Holton before shooting him and how did Johnny boy get cut up in the face? There were chunks of glass embedded and a nose so badly shattered it couldn't have been from when he fell forward from the shots."

"Well, Ostrow did yell 'drop it' but I could swear it was at the same time or just after he fired. As for the nose, my brave friend Norman attempted to disarm Holton while he was taking me out to die," said James, who was wondering whether Ostrow had acted under Marshall's instructions.

Mata surveyed the beer drinkers, zeroing in on Norman and Drea first.

"Let me guess—you would be the same Irishman who messed up our deceased drug dealers and you are the gringa Errol Flynn? This is your official notification to both retire from any such heroics in the future. Got it?"

Denise rose and reached out her hand. "We haven't met but we spoke on the phone, Detective. Denise Hamilton, *LA Times*. And this is Patrick Goldstein, also of the *Times*."

"I know who you are, Ms. Hamilton. That's the main reason I made sure I was standing close enough for you to overhear my conversation with Detective Ostrow. I'll give you everything I can as long as you guarantee you'll make it clear the corruption was in the sheriff's department and that Rampart brought it to light." Mata started to walk away but turned back.

"Your music column's not bad, Goldstein. I'm just glad you confine your grading every year to record labels and don't include police divisions…although you'd better watch your back. I hear some of those record company boys are killers."

"Now there's a thought, Detective."

CHAPTER 43

LA TIMES DECEMBER 9, 1980

CORRUPT DRUG DEALING DETECTIVE GUNNED DOWN BY HIS OWN PARTNER AT TROUBLED SILVER LAKE NIGHTSPOT.

SHERIFF'S DEPARTMENT TO INVESTIGATE. HOW DEEP DOES THE CORRUPTION GO? RUMORS OF NEW YORK MOB FAMILY INVOLVEMENT CURRENTLY UNSUBSTANTIATED.

BEATLE JOHN LENNON SLAIN: SHOT DOWN OUTSIDE NEW YORK APARTMENT BUILDING THE DAKOTA.

The phone rang and James put down the paper to go answer it. "It's me. Darby OD'd over the weekend. He's gone," said Drea.

⊕⊕⊕

NORMAN PICKED DREA UP, then collected James, and drove to Bogie's Liquor on Vine, where they acquired three bottles of Bell's Scotch, along with plenty of Rolling Rock beer.

They drove up Gower toward the recently renovated Hollywood sign, which, when James got to LA, was in crumbling disrepair. One of the *O*s had fallen off completely, which had actually been a better reflection of the state the city it topped was in.

They drove up Fuller to Runyon Canyon. It seemed a lifetime ago that he, Drea, and Darby had cabbed up to the Errol Flynn estate, and for Darby it really was. They unloaded the booze plus the essential boombox and traipsed through the crumbling edifices to the pool area with the aid of flashlights.

James loved the surreal, melancholy beauty of being in the decaying ruins of Hollywood's golden era, and it had felt like the right place to mourn their own lost souls.

He slid in the Psychedelic Furs cassette and "India" wound up its exquisite beginning before exploding against the rising moon.

Norman unscrewed his bottle, taking a long guzzle. "Jesus Christ. What a year it's been. And now we have a cheesy right-wing actor as president who wants to drag us back to a 1950s that probably never existed outside the movies anyway. How does that actually happen?"

"Not to mention an actor who sold out his friends to the House Of Un-American activities. I hate him," said Drea.

"I saw an episode of this TV series *World In Action* back in England, showing how marketing a president is done the same way as toilet paper," said James as the Furs sang, "America, ha ha ha."

"Maybe we should all go to London?" said Drea.

"Nah. As much as I loved London in my teens, don't think I'll live there again and definitely not while Thatcher's in. And fuck Ronnie Raygun. He ain't gonna drive me out. He's so fucking old anyway he'll probably keel over and die hopefully—or someone will off him too," said James.

Norman raised his bottle again. "Here's to John Lennon, man. The poor bastard didn't deserve to go down like that. It's a crying shame."

James wondered how Lauren Bacall was feeling, knowing the dullness at the Dakota would be changed forever. He had been avoiding facing the sadness closer to home but felt the Scotch start to work now and said, "So what the fuck happened to Darby? Last time I saw him for a night out, we were standing back-to-back on top of a table at Oki Dog, throwing shit at some punk jock poseurs and dealing with the reaction. A great fucking night, although I can't remember what had pissed us off about them in the first place."

"He planned to OD with Casey. He didn't give her enough but made sure he wasn't waking up. Did he ever tell you about his plan to do that and live out Bowie's 'Five Years'? With John Lennon dying the next day it's like no one fucking noticed," she said.

"No, he didn't. 'Rock 'n' Roll Suicide'? That's so fucking sad. He probably knew that wouldn't go down well with me. Don't get me wrong. It's still hard to imagine living to twenty-five, but somehow all these cunts coming after us this year have made me want to outlive them all. If this is the eighties, bring it on. Taking on all comers. The harder they come, the harder they fall. Fuck them all. What about you and smack, girl? It would be nice if you stuck around too."

She sighed. "Thanks to you, it's dried up, anyway, for now. And I would like to stick around. Maybe I'll find some new drugs for the eighties. You never know."

James realized in that moment that he would likely always live on the blurred edge of fact and fiction that was Los Angeles and that the ghosts of the misbehaving icons hovering around would spur them on to try to outdo them.

The Furs' "We Love You" started and the three of them screamed into the Hollywood night.

I'm in love with your blue cars
I'm in love with the words that scream
We are so stupid, we all dream
I'm in love with Frank Sinatra "Fly Me to the Moon"
I'm in love with fools like you
I'm in love with doing the twist
I'm in love with the bodies that scream
They fall so far, they fall so far
I'm in love with the Supremes
Oh, baby love

I'm in love with Sophia Loren

I'm in love with Bridget Bardot
I'm in love with the whole dumb scene
I'm so in love, you know what I mean
I'm in love with Althea and Donna
All that shit that goes, uptown top ranking

THE END

ACKNOWLEDGMENTS

Thank you for your help and support on this one:

Briana West	Mark Loquet
Adam Bennati	Karena Marcum
Mary Bergstrom	Janet McQueeney
Thea Constantine	Horace Panter
Darlene Caamano	Clark Peterson
Wayzate Camerone	The Psychedelic Furs
Anne Carey	Pilar Queen
Rebecca Choi	Katharine Ross
Wende Crowley	Jenny Ruskin
Ross Curtis	Elizabeth Pipin Silver
Rob Dillman	Genny Schorr
Steve Erickson	Roy Trakin
Glenn Feig	Dave Wakeling
Marie Ferro	Miki Warner
Jeff Freeman	Marc Wasserman
Nate Heller	Archer, for going into lockdown a
Maxim Karlik	year early with me to write this even
Josh Kun	though there's no English Springer
Francesca Lia Block	Spaniel in this one.

Thanks to the ones who were there at the O.N. Klub's beginning:

Aaron Paar

Julie Vaden

Bill Bentley

Jill Berliner

Sammy Carr

Jane Cole

Kim Cummings

Patrick Goldstein

Michael Goldstone

Carla Howard

Alan Jones

Norman & Patricia Lynas

Patrick Mata

Kalle Rikas

Sue Sawyer

Mitch Schneider

Bob Selva

Allan & Mary Seymour

Scott Sigman

Greg Sowders

Jeff Spurrier

Ann Summa

Perry Watts-Russel

Janet Van Ham

Ivan Wong

Howard Paar, a London native, created the O.N. Klub, the first ska club in the US, and subsequently worked as a longtime record label executive. Along the way he has worked with a wide array of iconic artists.

Today he is an award winning music supervisor and Academy member who has worked on over one hundred films and television series.

Top Rankin' is his second novel following 2015's *Once Upon A Time In LA.*